# DELTA RECON

## *SEAL TEAM PHANTOM SERIES*

## *BOOK 2*

### ELLE BOON

### Copyright © 2016

1

# Delta Recon
## Seal Team Phantom Series
## Book 2

By Elle Boon
elleboon@yahoo.com

© Copyright July 2016 Elle Boon

ISBN# **978-1537521275**

DELTA RECON, SEAL TEAM PHANTOM
SERIES BOOK 2
Copyright © 2016
ISBN: **978-1537521275**

# Dedication

I would like to thank the men and women who selflessly serve or have served in our military. It's because of you that we can rest, knowing you are protecting us near and far.

Of course I have to thank my family...my hubby who is my rock, my kids who are the most patient in all the world, never complaining when they have to fend for themselves when mama is writing for hours on end.

I'd also like to thank my Naughty Girls...y'all are the best team a gal could ask for. Without you and the others who help me, like Debbie, Trenda, Jenna, Annette, and Janet... all y'alls are #AHMAYZING. I would be a total mess without you. Y'all rock soo effing hard. Love y'all so hard <3

Last but certainly not least my fans aka you readers who are more friends than anything else. Without you I'd just be that crazy lady with funky hair. Love y'all sooo hard.

Elle Boon

# Chapter One

Jaqui Wallace swallowed the bile in her throat. She was an officer in the Navy for crying out loud. They didn't throw up or cry. Although looking around at her prison cell, she may rethink the former.

A rat the size of her neighbor back home's cat scurried across the dirt floor, its nose lifted, beady eyes looked at her as if she were its next meal, making her shiver. She fucking hated rats, but right then, she could imagine ripping its head off and eating it instead.

Again she swallowed, her hollow stomach had nothing in it to come back up, yet the image of eating the critter staring at her was enough to induce her muscles into spasms.

How long she'd been held without food she wasn't sure, wishing it was like in the movies where she at least had something to mark on the walls when a day passed. The scraps they'd brought her couldn't be classified as edible, but she knew it was only a matter of time before her survival instinct made her take what they offered. Each time she drank the dirty water they provided, her body paid the price in one or two ways.

"God, I no longer even smell the stench of my own shit," she whispered.

Hearing the sound of the guard's keys, she scooted to the far corner, close to where she'd been using as her makeshift bathroom. She may no longer smell it, but knew it was damn offensive to those who entered. Her body ached from the physical blows they inflicted, but she didn't allow them to see her cower.

"Eat," he said.

He held a bowl in one hand and a cup in the other, his one word demand came out in broken English. Jaqui kept her eyes on him, waiting for him to put the food on the ground and leave. It was the same every day, and each time she'd ignore the food, and water, until the gnawing was too great.

"Punta," he spat.

Yeah, she'd been called bitch, slut, whore and so many other things in the time she'd been their captive. Their words didn't hurt, not like the...she closed her eyes, not letting her mind go to what could and would probably happen when they got tired of waiting. She could feel the anticipation ramping up. For whatever reason they hadn't raped her. Yet. Her body had taken a few hits, nothing she hadn't expected. What she didn't know was how they found her. She wasn't even supposed to have been on the mission. The rest of the team had to know she'd been taken, even though they weren't supposed to be anywhere near her, surely they'd have had eyes in the vicinity.

The sound of metal clanging brought her back to the present. She sighed, looking at the dish on the ground and the little rat nosing around the food. Her mind snagged onto the possibility of feeding the critter and seeing if he survived.

"I'm pathetic." Survival of the fittest, and she was above the rodent. He almost fell into the dish, the greedy little bastard. When he finally stopped slurping at the slop, and didn't immediately fall asleep or fall over dead, she watched him, hoping he didn't go back out the way he came in.

Her stomach no longer growled in hunger, the pain a constant companion. "Alright you little fucker, the rest is mine. If it didn't kill you, then I guess it won't kill me." She'd started talking out loud to herself several days ago, the silence too deafening.

Upon the first taste of the goo, she swore it was the worst thing she'd ever eaten, yet she made herself eat the entire dish. What meat was in it would definitely be on the list of don't ask, don't tell. The flavor more salt than anything else, making her need to drink more of the putrid water. Which she realized after she'd drank the entire cup, was her mistake. Her head became heavy, the world started to spin, and in that moment, Jaqui wanted to kick her own ass. She tried to lift her hand and make herself throw up, but her body wouldn't obey her mind. The only saving grace was she had fallen far enough away from the bathroom corner. If she could have, she would've laughed.

She sent up a silent prayer, hoping her team found her before it was too late but a blessed fog came over her, then darkness.

Pain exploded in Jaqui's head, bringing her out of the darkness. Opening her eyes, she jerked back as far as the binding holding her would allow, banging her head against the hard back of a chair.

"Ah, I see you've decided to join us." A man said in heavily accented English.

She blinked a few times, the bright lights hurt after being in the dark for so long. "Who are you and what do you want?" Damn, even talking hurt. Her tongue felt three times too big, and drier than sandpaper, but she'd be damned before she asked for another drink.

The man laughed. "You do not ask the questions."

Giving him her best fuck off look, Jaqui shut her mouth, then wished she hadn't. The pain that had woken her had obviously been from someone hitting her in the face, splitting her lip open. She licked at the offending thing, and tasted her own blood.

"Now, tell me why you were asking questions about me?"

Her heart nearly stopped. She had been on a mission in Barranquilla, Columbia with a group of SEALs. Her job was to hack into the computers, not get into the thick of things. The last thing she remembered was watching the parade, and thinking it reminded her of Mardi Gras in New Orleans, only on a much much larger scale. She wondered where her team was, and if they were all being held like she was, or if they had escaped.

Her head rocked to the side as the man backhanded her. She couldn't help but wonder why men always resorted to backhanding, then decided a backhand was better than a fist to the nose. Her jaw hurt from the latest attack, making her wonder if he planned to permanently shut her up after making it impossible for her to open her mouth.

"I asked you a question, Miss Wallace. I suggest you answer, before my patience runs out. A pretty thing like you wouldn't want to have me as an enemy." He smiled, showing off a set of perfect white teeth, unlike the men who'd been her jailers for the past few days.

"I'm sorry, sir. I don't know what you're talking about." Her words came out a little garbled. She looked him in the eye, hoping he'd see honesty in her face.

He bent down, pinching her chin between his fingers. "Wrong answer. Do you know I am the only thing that is keeping you alive?" He squeezed harder. "Me. Look at you." He released her, walking away a few paces. "You won't survive the sport my men will play with you. What are you five foot two, maybe three? A hundred and ten pounds soaking wet? You won't last more than a day once they are through with you. Is that what you want?" He spun around and glared.

Jaqui shook her head, the pain had her stopping the motion at once. "I came here for vacation, to see the Carnival. It's known to be the largest in all the world. Me and my friends planned this vacation well

13

over a year ago. How was I to know you'd be here?" She hated the tremor in her voice. It was why she was not a field operative, but a computer tech.

He laughed. "That story has more holes in it than you will have. I'll tell you what. Since I'm in such a giving mood, and you stink worse than the pigs on a farm, I'll let you get cleaned up, then we will discuss this again." He wrinkled his nose. "Not even the lowest of my men would touch you in your present state. Diego, take her to the showers. If she gives you any trouble…knock her out and shower her clean yourself."

The man named Diego cut her arms loose, the burning sensation from having been tied up had her crying out before she could stop herself.

"Up, punta." Diego shoved the end of his rifle into her back.

Jaqui wobbled as she rose, the effects of the drugs, and sitting too long made her feel as if she'd just gotten off a spinning roller coaster.

"Oh, and Jaqui, don't get any ideas about running. This building is surrounded by my men, and the rainforest outside is filled with wild animals that are hungry for their next meal, even if you stink like they do." He turned and dismissed her.

In truth she had no idea where she was, let alone how to get out of her predicament. Her only hope was the men of Phantom Team were aware of her location, and they were launching a plan to get her back. It was a weak plan, but the only thing she had.

God, how she wished Tay were…she cut her thoughts off before they could form. He was the reason she was where she was. Having offered up her expertise when he'd been taken out, she knew the risks, sort of. In her naïve mind she'd assumed she'd be safe from the more dangerous aspects of a mission.

As they'd walked, she hadn't seen any other guards, her ears strained for voices to let her know how many more men or women were there. If she could get the gun from Diego, which in her present state she wasn't a hundred percent sure she could, she wasn't sure how many more she'd have to take out. Her next problem was knowing where she'd go if she succeeded in escaping.

The shower facility he led her to had three walls, and a concrete floor with a drain in the middle large enough she feared her foot would fall in it, or something large would crawl out.

Diego stood back, his eyes daring her to tell him to leave. Her filth was a layer of protection, but if she didn't clean herself, she knew without a doubt the bastard would.

Resigned, she turned the faucet on, putting her hand out to feel the water. Her mouth watered at the clear liquid coming out of the spout. She cupped her hands, catching some in her palms and drinking, uncaring her clothes were getting wet. Hell, she was filthy and going to be getting naked in front of this man, the last thing she was worried about was him seeing her with her clothes stuck to her body.

When she realized she could shower with her clothes on, she smiled with her back to Diego, using the little bar of soap on the ledge. Hell, her hair was a ratted mess, hanging to her ass that no amount of washing was going to get clean, or untangled, unless she had a good conditioner. She hoped her looks repulsed the fuckers, but at least she wouldn't smell like she'd rolled around in a pig's pen.

"Take off your clothes. You don't shower with them on," Diego ordered.

Jaqui froze with soap lathered up in her hands. She'd washed her face and under the tank top with the stuff, her hand reaching for her legs. "He didn't say I had to take my clothes off. I don't see a change of clothes."

"You will do as I say." He took a menacing step toward her.

The look in his eyes let her know he would be more than happy to help rid her of the soaking wet clothes.

Shouts rang out from the hall. The sound of gunshots followed by men yelling had Diego jerking toward the doorway, his body tensed. "Stay here."

She turned the water off, using the piece of cloth they'd left her to use as a towel and dried off as best she could. With nothing in the room to use as a weapon, she was a sitting duck if whoever was out shooting up the place came in.

17

Nerves stretched tight, keeping her back to the wall, Jaqui made her way to the door. The handle turned under her palm. She squeezed her eyes shut and prayed nobody was on the other side. Any minute she expected Diego, or one of the others to appear. Yet time stretched, and when the silence extended, so did her nerves.

Easing the door open, she peaked out. Bodies were strewn along the hallway. Blood soaking their clothing indicated the battle they'd fought. She walked back toward the office where the man in charge had been, stepping over a couple men, Diego's lifeless body lay a few feet from her destination.

She grabbed the gun from his hand, her training might not be on the same level as the men, but she knew how to use most weapons. She heard nothing beyond the closed door, but fear kept her from entering. A look to the left and right showed her at least ten dead men, which meant there had to be a survivor or two.

Her heart kicked beneath the drying shirt, the pounding was deafening to her ears. Mentally counting to five, she gripped the handle and turned. Inside the room where she'd been tied to a chair less than an hour before, was empty save for the furniture.

The reality of her situation hit her. The men who'd abducted her were dead, or had left amid the attack, leaving her stranded in the middle of nowhere. Her eyes landed on the desk. Papers on the top held no answers other than the local news. Jerking open the drawers afforded her nothing more. Panic threatened to send her to her knees, but then she remembered if they were getting local news, they couldn't be too far from where she'd been.

In the bottom drawer she found her bag, a feeling of relief was quickly wiped away when her cell wasn't inside. Shrugging her shoulders, she loaded up the few bottles of water she found in the mini cooler, checked the gun for bullets and headed for the door, only to stop at the sound of a vehicle.

Knowing if she was found alive in the middle of all the carnage, she had little to no chance of escape, she slipped out the window. Her feet hit the dry dirt soundlessly, jarring her back teeth from the long fall.

With her bag slung across her body, she ran toward the forest.

****

"What the hell?" Tay glared at the phone. He'd been ready to return to his team for the last two weeks, but hadn't been allowed because of the injuries he'd sustained from the last mission. They'd sent a little bit of fluff of a woman in to do his job. A woman he knew intimately, yet couldn't imagine her being held captive by the scums of the earth like Medellin.

"Don't take that tone with me, Taylor Rouland." Kai Swift growled. His tone hadn't raised, yet Tay could hear the leashed fury.

Taking a deep breath, he counted to ten. "What do you know?"

"She had a solid cover. Hell, the little condo she rented had three names listed, but she was taken right out from under the SEALs' noses. Medellin must've gotten inside intel with details of our mission, or at least part of it."

"Again, what are you doing now?" He looked around his apartment, calculating the time it would take him to get from Hawaii to Columbia, hating the fact their base was so far away.

"She's been gone for over twelve hours. We've been doing all we can to locate her, but she hasn't activated her PLB." Each member had a personal locator beacon, whether it was in a watch or on a piece of clothing, it only took a press of a finger, and their location would be pinged to their team leader.

"Fuck me man, tell me you have a backup plan." Jaqui was all of five feet two in her bare feet, and weighed in at a total of a hundred and fifteen pounds. She may be one tough woman, but she would be nothing against a man like him, or the drug dealers they were up against. Chauvinistic? Yes, he admitted he definitely was when it came to the woman in question. He'd seen her spar. Had gotten hard while watching her take on men twice her size, all the while he'd made a list of who he planned to beat the shit out of. His list had gotten shorter, while her sparring partners had also shrunk.

"We've narrowed down the location of Medellin to three possible sites. We'll be rolling out in the next hour, but I wanted to give you a heads up. I'll keep you updated." Kai sighed before continuing. "I'm sorry man. I can't tell you how pissed we all are."

He didn't care how anyone else felt, only that they'd lost Jaqui. Not wanting to investigate why her wellbeing was so important to him, he began gathering up things for his trip south of the border.

"I need transport like yesterday." He made sure Kai understood it wasn't a request.

"I assumed you'd say that. I also checked and found out you were cleared for duty. However, I need to ask how you are truly feeling. Oz is also cleared, but I haven't spoken to the big bastard yet."

Tay took one more look around his place. "I could be bleeding out, but I'd still be getting on a plane."

Kai's cursing could be heard through the line. "Yeah, I thought so. Your ride is waiting. See you soon."

As the line went dead, he sent up a prayer. If anything happened to Jaqui he'd never forgive himself. He didn't understand why she was with his team in the first place. Last he'd heard, she was shipping out to Afghanistan. Another thing he'd be getting answers for. With his laptop slung over his shoulder, he hopped into his jeep and raced toward the hangar. The faster he got to Bogota, the faster he'd find his answers.

Images of the last time he'd seen Jaqui popped into his head. God! He hated the hurt he'd caused her. His body ached to hold the one woman he couldn't have. She deserved a man who could offer her more than him. The weekend they'd spent together a year before had been the best damn two days of his life. Yet, he had left her lying on rumpled sheets with a promise to return.

She'd been a twenty-six year old virgin for crying out loud. He'd been a thirty year old man who'd seen and done things no woman would want to know about, let alone be with a man who'd done those things. He'd felt like he'd dirtied her more than just taken her virginity. Oh, he'd made sure it was good for her the two times they'd come together. And she'd been more than satisfied even though he knew she'd be sore when he finally let her sleep. It was when he'd woken in the wee hours, with the morning sun coming in through the window that he'd realized, sometimes when things seemed too good to be true, they were. She'd lain there smiling in her sleep, her long blonde hair looking like a halo around her head. The sheet had fallen away from her perfect breasts and he wanted her one last time. Bastard that he'd been, he'd almost taken her. Needing one last memory to hold onto. Had her phone not interrupted his sleep, he was sure he'd have made the biggest mistake of his life

He shook his head, clearing the memories away. Why the hell Commander Lee allowed her to go with his SEAL team he didn't know, but he'd make damn sure the fucker never made the same mistake again.

His hands balled into fists on his lap, the computer unopened.

Tay realized he hadn't once thought to check the files of the mission. If Jaqui had input anything in before her kidnapping he would be able to see it, and possibly trace her, or who she'd made contact with.

By the time they landed in a field on the outskirts of Cartagena, Tay was no closer to finding Jaqui. His eyes hurt from staring at the screen. His cell beeped, a message from Kai about his pickup. His eyes narrowed as he read the instructions.

"Thanks for the ride," Tay nodded at the pilot.

"Not a problem. Have a good trip." The two man crew watched him as he walked down the stairs. Tay felt the hairs on the back of his neck raise. With an inborn sense of survival, he ducked and rolled, pulling his SIG Sauer and fired off two shots toward the plane he just exited. The pilot's eyes widened before he jumped back into the cockpit. The other man returned gunfire, making Tay feel like a sitting duck in the middle of the open field. He wondered where his pickup was, and hoped like hell the pilot hadn't brought him to the wrong destination.

Kai's message lit up, the words "Big Black Jeep" and "Incoming Fast" gave him a boost of happiness. He lifted his gun and aimed just as the other man brought his arm out to shoot. The pain filled yell had Tay sprinting back toward the plane, using the man's distraction as his advantage. When he was close enough, he aimed and fired again in the vicinity he assumed the other man was hiding. A low grunt was his answer. With his back against the plane, and no longer in the middle of the field, he shot off a text to Kai explaining about the situation.

The roar of an engine wasn't as welcoming since he didn't know if it was his team, or another ambush.

He checked his clip and waited. "Fuck it." The sight of the big black jeep slowing down had him preparing for the worst, but hoping for the best. Coyle standing up with an AR15 aimed at the plane made him laugh out loud.

"You run into a little problem or what," Sully Griggs drawled, his own automatic weapon aimed at the plane. "You didn't tell us you were coming in hot."

Kai sat at the wheel with a man Tay had met before. Dallas Holt was a Navy Special Ops team member, but they'd never worked on the same team. He was known for his demolition skills, similar to Oz.

"You waiting on a special invite or what?" Kai looked at the plane and then at Tay.

Tay pointed to the open door. "There's a shooter inside. Not sure if the pilot is in on it or not."

Dallas grunted. "Well, we can jaw all night, or we can find out."

The tall man hopped down, rounded the front of the vehicle, his arms held loosely at his sides. Wearing black cargo pants and a black T-shirt that stretched across his wide chest, he looked more like a wrestler ready to do battle. He paused next to the steps, saluted Tay, then walked up the stairs.

"You might want to take a gun with you or something." Tay held out his own toward Dallas.

"I got my own," Dallas said, pointing to his back.

Kai stood next to the vehicle while Coyle had his weapon trained on the plane.

"I'd say this one ain't gonna be causing anyone any more problems." Dallas's voice carried from inside.

Tay went back up the steps, then stopped at the sight of Dallas squatting over the prone form of the male flight attendant. "I know I shot him in the hand and maybe the arm. How the hell is he dead?"

"Looks like he killed himself." Dallas shook his head.

"What about the pilot?" Tay felt the fine hairs on his neck standing up again. "Shit, we need to get the hell out of here."

Grabbing the man's ID out of his pocket, they both stood and ran for the door. "I'm thinking the pilot is either dead, or gonna be. Get out of here," Tay yelled.

Kai pulled the jeep up close and he hopped inside with Dallas on his heels.

"What the hell is going on," Kai asked.

Just as they reached the edge of the makeshift landing the ground rocked with an explosion.

"I assume that was a set up for all of us, or at least me." Tay fell against the seat.

"Oh, I don't know. We were supposed to have been there fifteen minutes earlier, but had a blowout nobody could have known about." Kai looked at him through the rearview mirror.

"I have one of the guys' ID, although I'm sure it's not his real one. Think you can figure out who he was?"

Tay nodded. "I'll see what I can do. My priority is finding Ace first."

Dallas looked at him. "Who the hell is Ace?"

"Jaqui Wallace, aka Ace to only a select few." Kai navigated through the trees.

"Have you anything new on her whereabouts?" He tried to keep the fear out of his voice.

Kai shook his head.

"One of you want to climb up front? It's a little tight back here for all of us," Coyle complained.

"Well if you didn't have to carry such a big ass gun, it wouldn't be so tight." Dallas elbowed Coyle, but climbed between the two seats upfront. His dark hair, cut military short and dark eyes made him fit in with the locals more so than Tay would. He and Kai with their coloring could fit into the culture without raising too many eyebrows, unlike him with his blond hair.

# Chapter Two

Jaqui ran like the hounds of hell were chasing her. Luckily for her, she was in shape and used to running miles on the daily. Unluckily for her, she had no shoes, and it was hotter than two squirrels humping in a wool sock in the desert.

Once she was certain she hadn't been followed, she slowed to get her bearings. Getting lost in the middle of the rainforest wasn't the smartest thing she could do. Getting dead though wasn't on her list of things to get done either. She hoped her PLB was still in her bag. The one in her watch she was sure was long gone, but the one discreetly disguised as a feminine product was her only hope. "Please be here," she begged.

The little feminine product holder was buried at the bottom of her bag. She was sure the men who'd gone through her stuff had probably seen it, and tossed it down like it was a rattlesnake. Pulling the two ends apart, she let the little female applicator fall unneeded inside, then pushed the locator button. A sigh of relief escaped her lips. Now, she just had to survive in the wilds until they sent a team out to find her.

A lone thought that her team had been ambushed, threatened to send her into a fit of tears, but Jaqui fought them back. "Should've worn big girl panties," she muttered and looked up to the sky. With all the overhead trees the sun was hard to see, but the heat still had her shirt sticking to her like a second skin. Now that she was no longer running, her feet were screaming. Lifting one, she saw it had a few cuts from her flight through the forest. Knowing her other foot would be just as bad made her grimace. A small cut could lead to a huge infection out in the climate she was in, not to mention her blood could be a call to the larger predators.

"Damn, I'm out of the frying pan, or whatever the hell the metaphor was," she mumbled as she looked inside her bag for something to clean her wounds. Antibacterial hand sanitizer and tissues, but nothing to bandage. "Why couldn't I have been a boy scout?"

After cleaning the wounds, she ripped a few strips off her shirt and wrapped them around her feet. Feeling like she'd accomplished all she could, Jaqui looked around her surroundings. The buzz of insects, chirping of birds, and other natural sounds surrounded her. Not once while she'd been held had she thought what it would be like outside the concrete walls. Thinking of all the indigenous creatures that would make a meal of her, she kept her back to the tree and waited.

Time crept by at a snail's pace. She drank sparingly from one of the bottles of water, wishing she had something to eat. "Rescue will be here in no time, and then you can get a big juicy steak back at the hotel." She kept her voice low, yet needed to hear something other than the oppressive silence.

Her back to one of the towering trees, she scooted down, allowing her ass to rest on her heels, the gun held loosely in her hands. Damn, why had they zeroed in on her? How many days had she been held hostage? She knew for sure it had been at least three nights. Seventy-two hours was plenty of time for a SEAL team to come up with a rescue plan, she was sure. God, she prayed they were enroute even now.

Aches she had forgotten about began to let themselves be known, her face hurt, her entire body felt as if it went three rounds with Conor McGregor. Only not in a good way.

Tiredness flooded her, making it hard to keep her eyes open. For the first time in days, the ability to sleep without the fear of what would happen to her, made it almost impossible to stay awake. Not even the oppressing heat, or the fact her clothes clung to her like a second skin made sleeping impossible.

It was the sound of the quiet that brought her to wakefulness. Darkness descended, making the already eerie forest even more so. Jaqui pushed to her feet, wishing she'd used the daylight hours to find a way out instead of assuming a team would come and rescue her. Now, with the silence, another danger was lurking. When she'd researched before coming on the mission, the main things had been about the Carnival itself and the city. Images of predatory animals flashed into her mind. Cats. She was sure it was large jungle cats of some sort, but couldn't put a name to which breed. Her eyes shot up to the towering trees as the realization that felines could climb, and would more than likely stalk their prey from above as well as from the ground.

The gun she felt secure in holding hours ago, didn't seem to hold much merit if a leopard or jaguar should appear. "Son of a bitch," she swore when she bit down on her bruised lip.

Taking a step away from the shelter of the tree, she tried to see through the foliage, hoping light from the moon would filter through. With the silence, she finally heard what sounded like running water. Knowing there were no waterfalls where she'd been, made anxiety twist her stomach in knots. If what she was thinking was true, she was no longer in Cartagena, and could be miles if not a country away from where she'd been. Hell, for all she knew, she could be in the Middle freaking East. Jaqui switched the gun to her left hand and used her right to steady herself, feeling her own heartbeat reminded herself she was alive. Water usually meant a couple things. One, she would be able to refill the water bottle she'd emptied if the water was fresh, and two,

the forest would open up enough for her to catch her bearings. On the downside, it also meant animals would also be near it.

Again, she wished exhaustion wouldn't have claimed her during the daylight, but unable to turn back time, she squared her shoulders. She was a good shot, and she hadn't survived this long only to succumb to a big cat.

Using her newfound reserve, Jaqui headed toward the sound of water. The closer she got, the louder it became, making her aware she wasn't near a small waterfall, but a huge one. As she broke through the clearing, the moon was already on the downside with the sun looking to make its appearance. For the first time in days her hope rose, until the sound of an animalistic growl split the air. The sound had the hairs on her arms rising. Jaqui looked at the area around the rushing waterfall, and back toward the trees.

"Stay calm. Surely there is other prey out there." Jaqui snorted, then pressed her battered lips together. Keeping close to the water, she made her way up, hoping she could get a better look from above. Her head jerked from side to side, trying to watch where she placed her feet as she climbed, yet keeping her eyes trained on where she was, sure she was being stalked. The last thing she wanted to do was shoot one of the local animals. However, survival was high on the agenda. If for nothing else, she planned to be able to throw it at Tay's...she shut her mind down, not wanting to think of him. The SEAL wanted nothing to do with her, and that was fine. She'd lost enough of herself because of her stupid infatuation with the man, she wouldn't lose anymore.

She was shocked at how out of breath she became by the time she'd reached the top. The fact she hadn't seen or heard anymore from the animal made her relax. She lifted her hand, the rushing water was almost deafening as it cascaded over the top. If she had been on vacation with friends, and a tour guide, this place would have been a must see sight. As it was, she felt more alone than ever. Why her locator hadn't brought in the troops made tears sting.

A large flat rock caught her attention, and with the last of her strength she climbed until she was on top. The short white shorts and cute top she'd put on for the first day of the Carnival mocked her. No longer resembling anything close to what she'd been wearing, the white was more shades of brown, and the top had no shape with the strips cut out. If someone was to come upon her, she was sure they'd think she was an escapee from somewhere. She wasn't even sure if her hair would ever be tameable, or if she'd have to chop it off. Why she was thinking these things, she had no clue. Exhaustion was the only thing that came to mind.

Once the sun was up, she planned to figure out the correct direction and make plans. Uncapping a bottle from her bag, she drank deeply. She wasn't paying attention, or she'd have noticed the silent wraith creeping up on her. Her first warning she wasn't alone was the eerie feeling of being watched, or stalked.

Slowly, she glanced up and over her shoulder, seeing the large creature not five feet away. If her memory served her correctly, it could easily clear that distance. With an economy of movements, she reached into the bag, keeping her eyes locked with the cat. The gun felt good in her palm, but she feared if she pulled it out too quickly, he'd be on her. Yet, if she waited he'd be on her.

She finally understood what they meant when people said time stood still. In the moment before her hand came clear of the bag, she had the safety off and her other arm up, ready to help steady for the shot. The scream from the jaguar scared her, almost making her scream herself. She wanted to tell the gorgeous beast to go away, but reasoning with an animal would be a waste of time. Jaqui paused, waiting for the subtle shift in his body. Just as the bunching of its muscles flexed, she pulled the trigger. A terrifying scream ripped from the jaguar, but he still leaped at her. She fired again, and again.

Falling over backward, the heavy weight of the animal bore down on her. Jaqui screamed, and screamed some more as she pulled the trigger. The animal's huge head was inches from biting her, and then it dropped, half on, half off her. Its deadly claws looked vicious even in death.

Jaqui tried to scramble out from under the animal, its blood covering her, along with everything else, was enough to make her lose control and scream until she was hoarse. She didn't care that others would hear her, if there were more in the area, only knew she was too tired to care.

The rising sun no longer held a promise of rescue, or safety. Her body began to shake uncontrollably, yet she couldn't seem to get her legs out. The jaguar's large head mocked her as she lay there, shaking, screaming until her throat hurt, until her limbs went numb. Finally, she released her hold on the gun, letting it drop beside her. "I'm done," her voice came out scratchy, barely above a whisper.

\*\*\*\*

Tay swore in several languages when they'd heard the echo of gunfire. The tracker Jaqui had pressed had been found, yet no sign of the woman. Now, as they raced through the forest toward the ominous sound of shots, he prayed. He prayed like he hadn't since he couldn't remember when. Even with the night vision goggles, he worried about what they couldn't see. The thought that little Jaqui Wallace was stranded with nothing but her wits had him freaking the fuck out, and he wasn't ashamed to admit it. If the last thing he did on this earth was save the tiny blonde beauty, then he'd die a happy man. If one hair on her gorgeous head has been hurt, he swore he'd make each and every person responsible wish they were already dead.

He leapt over some fallen trees, leading the team even though it was Kai's place. They all knew he had feelings for the Navy's computer specialist. What he didn't understand was why she was allowed to come out on a mission with his SEAL team. No way in hell was she trained for the things they might encounter. He grunted as his legs ate up the distance where they were sure the shots had come from. He wouldn't allow himself to think she wasn't still alive. The gunfire had sounded as if it'd come from one gun, not several.

"Yo, Tay. Slow your roll man. Check this out." Kai pointed at some markings on a tree at the base of the forest where it opened to a huge waterfall. "Looks like some sort of large jungle cat, man. Keep your eyes open."

Tay nodded, his eyes looking up and down along the water's edge. Surely she hadn't jumped in to escape the animal chasing her?

"We split up. Half go up, half go down." Kai checked his gear. "Tay and I'll go up. If you see anything give three clicks on the radio."

He already began searching as he went up. The first sign of footprints had him nearly dropping to his knees in relief. "Kai, check it out. She went up."

Picking up his pace, he moved quickly upward, eyes and ears open for any sign of Jaqui. Just as he was about to reach the top, his heart nearly stopped. A huge jaguar lay sprawled on top of what appeared to be a woman with long hair. He couldn't tell the color of the locks, yet something in his gut told him it was his Jaqui. Blood coated both beast and woman, yet neither moved.

"What the hell, Tay," Kai growled, almost bumping into him from behind.

His body moved on autopilot, moving closer to the two on the ground. He heard Kai swearing, heard his order to stand down, but Tay wasn't listening. The closer he got, his mind went back to the weekend he'd spent with Jaqui.

*Tay stared at the vision in front of him, unable to believe she was agreeing to spend the weekend with his sorry hide. Jaqui Wallace was everything his mama would want in a wife, a forever kind of girl for her son. She was exactly what he should be running from, instead of renting a suite for the weekend.*

*Her long blonde hair was pulled back in a ponytail, its long thick mass gave him fantasies of things a good boy shouldn't be having about the girl next door. But, the look she gave him wasn't one he'd ever seen on any of the neighbors back home. In fact, he was sure not a man alive could resist her sweet temptation wrapped in a tiny package.*

*"Why are you looking at me like that?" she asked. They were inside the elevator and as he moved to cover her lips with his, the doors opened.*

*Shaking his head, he reached for her hand with his free one, gripping the handle to her overnight case in the other, he led the way down the hall toward their room. Damn, butterflies took up residence in his stomach. At thirty, Tay was amazed at the reaction.*

*"Wanna do the honors." He tilted his head toward the key card slot. A blush rose on her tan complexion. At twenty-six it was an endearing thing to see. He wanted to test her, see what she looked like naked and if that blush would cover her entire body. He'd bet his last dollar it did.*

*After a failed attempt, they both seemed to hold their breaths until the little green light indicated the door was unlocked. Walking inside, the room wasn't too large, but it was much nicer than the average hotel room. Not wanting to rush things, he left the bags near the couch, then turned to look into the eyes of the woman who'd captivated him from the first time he'd seen her. Having just returned from a mission, he'd wanted to relax on the beach. With his team's home being in Hawaii, he couldn't wait to shed his fatigues, and hit the beach. He had no clue how he'd missed seeing her on the Navy base, but as he paddled out to catch a wave, his eyes landed on the tiny female racing alongside him. He'd have thought she was trying to impress him, except she'd paid no attention to him, and caught the first wave. Lust at first sight was what he'd called it.*

*Now, he stared at her in the yellow sundress, and wondered why he was so nervous. "Do you want to go out and grab some dinner?" He asked hoping to set them both at ease.*

*She shook her head.*

*"Want to order room service, or take a walk and see what catches our eye?"*

*Again she shook her head, then did something he'd never forget. Raising her hands, she slipped the strap of the dress off one shoulder, then the other. Her small, but perfect breasts stopped it from falling until she hooked her thumbs in the material. With her eyes locked on his, she shimmied, taking the yellow fabric all the way till it passed her hips, then let it drop to the floor unheeded.*

*"Have mercy." He swallowed, and erased the few feet separating them. She wore a pair of yellow bikini panties, and a white strapless bra with yellow lace to match the panties.*

*He lifted his hand, tracing the edge of the lace. "Fuck, you are the most beautiful thing I've ever seen. You make the sun pale in comparison."*

*A dimple appeared in her right cheek as she smiled. "Nice line, soldier."*

*"Don't do that. You have to know you're gorgeous." He wrapped one arm around her back, cupping the back of her head in his palm, he stared*

into her eyes. *"Yeah, I've given lots of women a line of BS, but not you. I won't lie to you, or promise anything I can't deliver."*

*Using the hand near her hair, he gripped the long ponytail, and gave a tug when she didn't agree right away. When her smile reappeared, he swore the sun became brighter.*

*"Now, do you want to get dressed and eat something before I show you just how much I want you? Cause make no mistake, I want you more than a man on death row wants a pardon."*

*She laughed. "That is so not romantic, Rouland."*

*With one hand cupping her rounded ass, the other her head, he brought her body flush to his. "You're lucky I'm able to string more than grunts and curse words together. Damn, having you in these little bits of silk and lace are enough to make a saint a sinner, and baby, I'm far from a saint."*

*Her hand lifted and for the first time, he needed a woman to touch him. The tentative touch lit up his nerves. Slowly, she ran the tips of her fingers over the* exposed flesh from his V-neck T-shirt. His cock, already hard as a baseball bat, jerked beneath the confines of the denim. "Kiss me, Tay."

His head dipped, a soft brush of lips and then he lost all meaning of time. Her sweet lip-gloss coated his mouth by the time he lifted his head. Both of their breathing was choppy. She stood in a pair of wedge heels and her lingerie, while he was completely dressed. A fact that kept him from shoving the little scrap of fabric from her, and shoving his dick inside without a care in the world, other than blowing his load. They'd kissed many times, but never with the knowledge they'd be getting naked shortly. Tay had always pulled back, going back to his own place and rubbing one out with a picture of her in his mind.

He bent and picked her up like the precious thing she was, and carried her into the bedroom, glad he'd chosen the deluxe suite with the king bed. Resting her weight on his leg and with one arm, he jerked the cover back, then placed Jaqui down. The pristine white a perfect foil for her coloring.

*His mouth watered at the thought of tasting every delectable inch of her. "Look at you. So effing sweet laid out like that, you make my teeth ache."*

*"Got a sweet tooth do you?" She raised her hand, waving him toward her with the crook of her finger.*

*Reaching behind his head, he tugged the T-shirt over his head, loving the sigh that escaped her throat.*

*"What was that for?" He asked as he tossed his shirt on the chair.*

*"I think it's sexy as all get out when men do that tug over their head from behind thing with their shirts."*

*The thought of her watching other men almost made him lose his shit. He didn't want her thinking of any man but him. "Hmm, seen lots of men undress have you?"*

*Her smile grew. "I've watched Magic Mike XXL like ten times. For educational purposes you understand."*

*Tay shook his head, dropping his chin to his chest to shield his eyes. No way could he let her see*

49

*the mirth in his expression. Pulling out his cellphone, he pulled up his playlist, and found what he was looking for. As soon as the song began playing, he placed the phone on the nightstand. With a roll of his hips, he started dancing, mimicking the moves of a male stripper. Her eyes watched him and his fingers while he unsnapped his jeans to the beat. He'd of course seen the movie she'd mentioned with a woman he had taken out a few times. However, he'd never done an impromptu strip tease for anyone. Once the zipper was down, he spread the sides apart, giving his hard cock room to breathe.*

*"Oh, no commando for you," she teased.*

*Rolling his hips, he spun around and wiggled his hips. He pushed the jeans down his thighs slowly, bending at the hips and looking over his shoulder to see Jaqui's expression. Her wide-eyed gaze and tongue flicking out to lick her lips, had him grinning.*

*He was no Channing Tatum, but he did know how to dance. The tip of his dick peeked out of the top of his boxer briefs, mocking him and his need to tease. Hell, if he kept it up, he'd need to take a cold shower before joining her on the bed. Filling his lungs with air, he turned around, but left the briefs on. A man only had so much restraint, and his was at the limit.*

*Gentlemen never raced to the finish line, only to leave theirs partners behind. And Taylor Rouland was raised a gentleman.*

*"I prefer something between me and my jeans," he murmured placing one knee on the bed. "Unless it's getting in the way of me and you, then me and Junior can't stand it."*

*"You call that Junior?" She pointed at the part of his body straining the cotton briefs.*

*Crawling over her prone form, he placed a knee on each side of her thighs. "Yep, he's a little me. I swear, sometimes he does the thinking, and right now he's screaming to get out."*

*She reached out her right hand, lightly toughing the tip with one finger. Tay couldn't help the full body shiver. Before her hand could be pulled back, he placed his over hers, coiling her fingers around the base.*

51

*Her gasp was swallowed by him as he closed the distance between their mouths. God, he could get used to her responses. Her blush did indeed turn the golden tone of her skin a becoming shade of red. Needing to see every inch of her, he wasted no time in taking off the sexy bra, dropping it over the side of the bed. Her panties went next, leaving only his briefs between them.*

*He took his time savoring every inch of her body, kissing down her neck, nibbling on the slopes of her breasts. When he sucked the tip of one hardened nipple into his mouth, she nearly bucked him off. Damn, he was one lucky bastard.*

*His fingers trailed down her flat tummy, zeroing in on the neatly trimmed patch of blonde curls. He'd love to see her pussy bare, and watch the way her face lit up the first time those nerves were exposed. Slipping through the slick folds, he was pleased to find smooth skin. Sweet little Jaqui had a naughty side and he couldn't wait to explore every inch and facet of her.*

The tight little bud at the top of her pussy begged for attention. Using his thumb, he pressed down, then ran it around in a circle before dipping lower into her tight entrance.

"You're so wet. Hot. Fuck, I can feel you tightening on my finger already," he groaned.

She lifted her hips, trying to force him to do more. Tay wanted, needed to taste her first.

"Please, I need..."

"Ssh, I know what you need. Let me take care of you," he said, giving her another kiss. This time he sucked her lower lip between his, giving it a little bite and then letting it go.

Working his way down, he sucked one nipple into his mouth, using his body to hold her down when she jerked upward again. He did the same to the next, sucking, licking and nibbling on the hard tip, soothing the little hurt with a swipe of his tongue. Continuing down, he nipped and licked, moving his body between Jaqui's quivering thighs.

*"Holy crap, I feel like I'm going to shake apart."*
*Her voice shook on each word, A slight tremor rocked*
*her beneath him.*

*"I've got you." He looked up, catching her stare.*
*"I'll always be there to catch you."*

*The fingers of her right hand lifted, her pale pink*
*nail polish sparkled in the setting sun streaming*
*through the window. "I know. I trust you, Tay." She*
*ran her hand over his close cropped hair.*

*Unmanned. He would do his damnedest to be*
*worthy of that level of trust. Not thinking too hard on*
*the future, he concentrated on the here and now. The*
*woman and her sweet pussy.*

*Spreading the folds hiding her from him, he*
*stared at Jaqui while he reached out with his tongue.*
*Licking firmly around the bundle of nerves, he*
*replaced his thumb with a finger, then added another.*
*Within minutes her abrupt movements and pleas had*
*him pumping the digits faster, and then he sucked her*
*clit into his mouth, making her scream his name.*

*"Oh god, Taylor. Yes, right there. Don't stop."*
*Her thighs clamped around his head, holding him in place as her inner muscles spasmed.*

*When he was sure she'd finished, he sat back on his heels. "You taste delicious." He licked first one, then the other finger clean, making a sucking noise with each one.*

*"Taylor Rouland," she moaned.*

*Yep, that blush was back and he fucking loved it. Climbing off the bed, he shucked his briefs, reaching into his jeans for the condoms he kept there. Two, he stared at the small squares, then at the woman. He'd need to get his bag, cause he knew as sure as he knew the sun rose in the east and set in the west, there'd be more than a few rounds this night.*

*Sheathing himself, he turned to see Jaqui staring at him. "Like what you see, darlin?"*

*An uncertain look crossed her face, but she nodded.*

*"Hey, if you've changed your mind we can stop." It'd kill him, and he'd definitely be visiting the bathroom for a little one on one hand time.*

*She licked her lips. "I've not changed my mind. Make love to me, Tay."*

*He almost corrected her and told her he didn't make love, but with Jaqui it was different than with other women. They'd been dating for a couple months, yet he'd not pressured her into sleeping with him. Something held him back. Not that he didn't want her, and ache like a mofo at the end of their dates. However, there was a need to be more. To know more about her, and explore a real relationship. Usually he was running for the hills when a woman brought up emotions. He shook his head, clearing it of all thoughts of everything, except Jaqui and him now.*

*"I'm glad," he agreed.*

*Moving back between her spread thighs, he braced himself on both elbows next to her head. "Hi," he whispered, and then kissed her eyes closed. She'd tensed up and that was the last thing he'd wanted. Feathering kisses along her high cheekbones, on the corners of her mouth, and then finally sealing their lips, he let their tongues mimic the act their bodies would be doing.*

*He kept his weight off her body for the most part, but then she lifted her legs, pulling him down onto her. The feel of her hard nipples against his chest was an added sensation he had never thought he'd enjoy, but with her he was finding all kinds of firsts.*

*The warm wet heat of her pussy kissed his stomach, making his cock jerk where it lay next to her thigh. He couldn't help the involuntary movement of his hips as he rubbed back and forth, the sweet friction not enough.*

*She turned her head away, breaking their kiss. "Need you in me."*

*Reaching down between their bodies, he tested her readiness, happy to feel the wetness of her arousal coating her. He played with her a little, then knowing he wouldn't last much longer, grabbed his cock. Tay ran the latex covered tip through her slit, then pushed inside.*

*"Fucking hell. So tight." He squeezed his eyes shut, pulling back and then moving forward. The cold*

*air from the air conditioner, did nothing to cool him down as he worked his way inside the tightest thing he'd ever had the pleasure of entering. Finally when he was balls deep, he stopped, resting his forehead on hers. "You okay?" Shit, if he didn't know better, he'd swear she was a virgin.*

*"Yeah, just give me a minute."*

*He waited while she relaxed one muscle at a time it seemed. "Take all the time you need." Not wanting to let her or him wait too long, he lifted up a little. The passion from moments ago no longer reflected back at him. Unacceptable. He bent enough to take one of her sensitive nipples into his mouth, hardening the tip of his tongue, he played with the little bud. Releasing the right breast, he kissed a wet path across her chest, then paid the same homage to the left. The feel of her moisture coating his cock was a welcome relief. One he was more than happy to take advantage of.*

*With a wet pop, he lifted his head. Experimentally, he pulled his hips back, then pushed back in. Jaqui made a soft sound, her hand ran over his shoulder, around his neck.*

*His own hands itched to tangle in her locks. Unable to hold still any longer, he began a slow glide, her body's moisture making it easier. She gasped, arching up. Tay dropped his face into the crook of her neck, sucking a bit of flesh between his lips. She was even better than he'd imagined, her small body was tight, stretching to accept him. He loved the fact she was so much smaller than him, yet their bodies were perfect together.*

*He pushed up onto his hands, pushing her thighs farther apart, moving his hips in tight circles.*

*Jaqui's legs wrapped around his, wiggling beneath him, making him move in deeper circles, being sure to hit her clit on each pass. He felt her inner muscles begin to tighten, squeezing down on him. Her groan was music to his ears, entrancing him as she tossed her head from side to side, the way her hair practically danced beneath and around her head.*

*He slid his knees farther apart, forcing her wider, making her lose the grip on his legs with her shorter legs. With his weight braced on his knees, and one arm, he reached under her narrow hip and lifted her into his thrusts. Wanting to feel her come around him one more time, he reached for the bud at the top of her pussy. He pinched it between his thumb and forefinger, not hard, but enough to make her cry out and that sweet blush stole over her chest. She tightened around him, screaming his name, dragging him over the edge with her.*

*"Shit, yes. So good, baby." He buried his face in her hair, biting his lip to keep from saying anything stupid.*

*He'd never had his eyes actually roll into the back of his head like they did when he'd came moments ago. Even now his hips continued to thrust. It was as if each tremble, each tremor of her body had his own doing the same. A slight regret that he had to wear a condom, instead of feeling her skin kissing his cock made him pull back. Tay lifted his head to see a sultry look on Jaqui's face.*

*His body tensed as he prepared to pull out, and then she pulled his head down for a kiss. The kiss light, almost questioning. In that moment he'd have agreed to anything. The depths of his feelings shocked him into disengaging their bodies. "Let me get rid of this." He rolled to the side, then hopped up. As he stared at his reflection in the mirror, he was sure he'd made a huge mistake. How would he be able to walk away from the woman who owned half his soul if not more?*

*Not wanting to dwell on it, he looked down at the used condom to make sure it hadn't broken. The sight of the red smears made him do a double take. His hands shook while he tossed it into the garbage and then ran warm water over his face.*

*Damn it. Why was she still a virgin at twenty-six years old? And more worrisome. Why did she waste such a precious gift on him? Tay needed to make sure she understood he was not a forever kind of man. He was a Navy SEAL. His team and country came first and last in his world. He didn't have the time or energy to be in a relationship. With his mind firmly made up, he walked back into the room. The setting sun made the room look almost magical, a small beam of the last ray the only bit of light, yet it was enough that he swore she looked like a goddess laying with the white sheet pulled up to her hips. Lying on her side, her eyes ate him up.*

*Her nipples beaded under his stare. The slight shift of her legs made the sheet dip a little lower, exposing the smooth and rippled abs of her stomach. Jaqui was more than just fit, she was a soldier. Surely she hadn't been saving herself for him, but hadn't had time to find a man who she felt comfortable with. He nodded, his legs taking him across to the bed before he'd realized that was where he wanted to be.*

*She surprised him on so many levels, but none so much as when she stood, and pushed him onto his back. Tay was sure his eyes rolled into the back of his head for the second time as Jaqui took her time exploring him. Grabbing a condom, he rolled it on, unable to take anymore, he gripped her narrow hips in his palms and lifted her onto his cock.*

*"Jumping Josephite," he swore. He forced her onto him, the slick wet heat of her made his entry a little easier this time.*

*Jaqui moved with the sensuous grace of a dancer, her strong thigh muscles bunching and flexing as she lifted, only to fall back down. He groaned as she moved faster and faster, the silk of her pussy caressing his cock had him close to coming. Tay tried to slow her movements, knowing he wasn't going to last. He tensed, moments from spilling his come.*

*Her back bowed as she leaned back, giving him access to the little cluster he knew would make her go off like a rocket, or at least he hoped it did. Running his finger around in it, he gathered some of her sweet arousal.*

*"Yes. Tay, fuck me harder."*

*Grinning he continued to flick his finger over the bud. His hips lifting and falling. Her body began gripping him, his balls ready to spill his load and Tay did just what the lady asked, grabbing her hips and took over. Moving her up and down, faster, harder, racing toward the sweet release he needed. This time when they came, their breaths were both ragged, and when Jaqui collapsed on him, he wrapped his arms around her.*

*His dick twitched inside her. "Tell Junior he needs to take a break," she murmured around a yawn.*

*He chanced a quick look down, but her eyes were closed. The deep even breathing let him know she slept. Never had he ever wanted to stay in bed and think about forever with a woman before. The sound of a phone vibrating caught his attention. He eased out from under Jaqui, knowing both of them needed to check their phones in case of an emergency. Since his was on the nightstand he assumed it had to be hers and went to retrieve it.*

*The message from her friend Summer that popped up had him freezing in his tracks.*

*"Hey girl. Hope you lost your V card to the man you love. I expect an invite to the wedding."*

*He looked at the phone and then at the sleeping woman in the bed. Thoughts swirled in his head. Had she thought he'd marry her if she gave him her "V* card" like her friend stated? *Shit!* He needed to get out of there and get some air.

Grabbing up his discarded clothes, he quickly got rid of the condom and quietly dressed. Before he left, he scribbled a note on the hotel notepad, thinking he'd be back in a few hours.

# Chapter Three

God, if he could go back to that night and return, instead of running away like a coward, he would. Now, he held his weapon in front of him, preparing to shoot the animal. He circled the pair, heart racing. Every part of him wanted to jump onto the spotted back of the jaguar.

The man in him wanted to rush forward and check the woman, but the soldier held back, securing the perimeter. Tay took a deep breath, forcing calm to settle over himself to fight off the rising fear. He'd get nowhere or dead real quick if he acted rashly. Up close he couldn't see the rise and fall of the cat's body.

Kai stayed back, his presence reassuring. They needed to hurry, but his leader was giving him a chance to adjust to what they were seeing.

"The jaguar's dead," Tay said. He swung his rifle around on his shoulder, the familiar move done without him having to think about it.

He looked over his shoulder, but it wasn't worry in Kai's eyes. It was pure unadulterated rage. The same anger burned in his gut. Pushing everything to the side, he bent and felt the first bit of relief wash over him as he found a pulse beating in the outstretched arm of the woman. He had to move the dirty hair off the woman's face, but he knew it was Jaqui. With the dead animal lying on her, the two hundred pound animal had to be squishing her. "Help me get him off her." Tay deliberately turned his head toward the job at hand. He and Kai rolled the cat off, seeing the bullet wounds showed them how she'd protected herself.

The unmoving woman who they came to rescue was too pale. Tay gave up on not looking. He squatted down, brushing the dirty hair away from her bruised and bloodied face.

"Fucking hell," Kai growled.

The urge to kill rose up swift and hard. "We need a Helivac, Kai."

Kai looked around. "We'll have to carry her some distance to find a clearing even for that. Let's check her injuries."

Tay sighed. His mind knew he was right, but his heart didn't want to waste a minute. While Kai ran his hands from foot to head, checking Jaqui for breaks, he stood guard, watching her face for any sign of distress. As the seconds became minutes, and her breathing didn't change, worry replaced fear.

"I don't feel anything broken, but I can't say if she has any back or neck injuries. It could be too dangerous to carry her over your shoulder. We could build a stretcher, but I'm thinking her problem isn't that. She has a lump on the back of her head." Kai pulled Tay's hand around, letting him feel the large lump. "We need to move her out with as little fuss as possible. We also don't know for sure if Medellin had her or not. I can guarantee you if he did, he's not happy she escaped."

He pinned Kai with a hard stare. "I'll kill the son of a bitch if he comes after her again."

Kai nodded. "I figured you'd say that, which is why I need you to keep your shit together and focus on Jaqui. This mission has gone south, and not just in destination. We weren't here to stop drug trafficking, but to find out if the cartel was into human trafficking. I hate to think Jaqui may have stumbled into something she shouldn't have, and is now a target."

Noise behind them had he and Kai spinning, guns up before either man could say a word.

"Damn, what happened to our girl?" Sully moved with silent grace, ignoring Tay's glare, he knelt next to Jaqui's head and checked her over. "Her pupils grow smaller when I shine my light in them. See?" Sully lifted each eyelid again, demonstrating what he meant.

"We need to get to higher ground. I can get us a ride out of here, but through all these trees." Kai's arm swept out in an arc.

The huge towering things surrounding them did more than just provide the perfect cover for drug traffickers, but it also made it difficult for them to get an injured soldier out. "She'll be okay, man." Coyle's deep voice broke into his thoughts.

"I'll carry her." Tay dared any of them to deny him his right. When nobody said a word, he carefully lifted her into his arms. She'd lost weight since the last time he'd held her. Forcing himself to not think about that time, he took up a position in the middle of his team.

The pace Kai set was brisk, but nothing like what they'd usually do. They were all taking into consideration their injured team member. The low moan had his heart clenching.

"It's okay, Jaqui. I've got you," he whispered down, hoping he wasn't jarring her too much. He'd wanted to use the water they had and clean some of the blood and dirt from her face, but out in the field they needed to conserve…just in case. Now, he wondered just how badly she'd been hurt. Thoughts of what she'd endured almost had him stumbling.

"Is she waking up?" Sully asked.

"No. I think moving her is hurting even in sleep. We don't know what those fuckers did while they had her for three motherfucking days." His arms squeezed a little tighter, his voice a mere rasp, but he never faltered in his steps.

Kai's eyes glittered as they looked over his shoulder. "We'll get them."

At the top of the waterfall a river flowed, but there was more than three feet of clearing, enough for a helicopter to land. That was all Tay needed in order for Jaqui to get lifted out.

The unmistakable sound of womp, womp, womp, could be heard, and in that moment he knew he'd have to hand his burden over to someone else's care.

"She'll be alright. We need to finish our mission, Tay." Kai's dark eyes looked from him then to the man waiting by the helicopter.

He was furious and wanted vengeance for what was done to Jaqui, and all the others who had suffered beneath the cartel. Instead of handing Jaqui into the outstretched arms, he climbed into the back and lay her onto the stretcher. "You make sure she is taken care of like she's the most precious thing in the world. Tell Commander Lee I want to be notified as soon as she wakes. Feel me?"

They looked at the blood covered woman, and then him who was now covered in blood as well and nodded.

Tay put his lips to Jaqui's ear and murmured too low for anyone else to hear how sorry he was, and promised to make it up to her. He begged her to be okay, and told her he'd kick everyone's ass who'd hurt her. Then he kissed her bruised and swollen cheek before standing.

"She's a SEAL, boys. Remember that." He made sure he looked at each man, memorizing their faces. He wanted them to know he would make sure they were held accountable for her wellbeing from this point on.

When he climbed out, his team stood there with equal looks of fury radiating off of them.

"Let's go hunting, men." Tay swung his gun around.

A round of *Hooyah* were growled out.

\*\*\*\*

Jaqui woke up with a start. The unfamiliar room and beeping had her trying to sit up, then she cried out as pain rocked her from her head to her toes. She couldn't move her arms, which freaked her out until she realized she was strapped down, then she panicked.

"Oh no. Please God, no," her voice didn't sound like her own. It hurt to say those few words, and tears she didn't want to shed flowed from her eyes.

Her eyes jerked open as a woman entered. "You're awake. Thank the lord. I've already alerted the doctor on call. How are you feeling? Oh, silly question. Can I get you anything?"

Holy shit, was this woman for real? "Thirsty." Jaqui moved her fingers, hoping the woman would release her.

After she had her vitals checked, and Jaqui was ready to claw the perky lady's eyes out, a man dressed as a doctor came in, and still she'd not gotten a drink, or been released.

"Hello, Ms. Wallace. I'm Dr. Davalari. I'm more than pleased you finally decided to wake up." He came to stand next to the bed. "Molly, let's get these restraints off of her. I don't think she'll try to hurt herself again."

His words made no sense. Her last memory was of the large jungle cat jumping on her. Jaqui was sure she was going to die in the middle of the jungle beneath a freaking animal, after being beaten by a drug dealer. Hell, they made Lifetime movies after ordeals like hers.

As the straps were released, she immediately wanted to rub her wrists, but IV lines in one had her pausing, while swelling and bruising on the other made her take a long look.

"How long have I been here?" It couldn't have been too long since her bruises weren't fading.

A pen light was held in front of her face, and she followed directions, while what she really wanted was water.

Her tongue came out, licking dry cracked lips.

"Ah, would you like something to drink?" He reached for the cup with the straw in it from the nurse.

Looking from the doctor to the nurse, Jaqui allowed him to place the straw in her mouth and took a sip. Her first instinct was to spit it out, worried about being drugged, but the refreshing liquid felt too good on her tongue, she sucked harder.

"Where am I?" She asked when he pulled the cup back, staring at the tray holding the water.

"Not too much at once. We don't want you getting sick." Dr. Davalari performed a few tests she knew were all normal, but her mind didn't feel like it was functioning properly.

When she heard the word concussion, and Walter Reed, Jaqui finally let her body relax and cried. If she was at Walter Reed, then she was in the United States and that meant she was safe.

"How?" The one word came out as a croak.

Dr. Davalari shook his head. "You'll have to ask your superior. I'm to inform him as soon as you woke up, which I've already done. Now, let's go over your injuries."

She listened as he rattled off the fractured zygomatic bone, or her cheekbone from Jose Medellin's fist. The bruised ribs from being crushed under a two hundred pound jaguar, and other deep tissue bruises that would all take time to heal.

Not to mention the fact her face looked like she had gone two or three rounds with a boxer. Or so the good doctor said. She had a fuzzy memory of Tay whispering in her ear, but that couldn't be right. He'd been in the U.S., while she'd been in the middle of godforsaken Columbia. A shudder wracked her, making her cry out before she could stop herself.

"Try not to move too much." The tone was gentle as he shone a light in each of her eyes again, making her wince. "I'd say you were very lucky, Ms. Wallace, your pupil dilations are all normal."

Jaqui blinked up at him. If he thought being beaten by men twice her size, then chased through the jungle, first by men, and then a freaking jaguar…then yeah, she was lucky. Of course, she was alive to tell the tale. Maybe she'll make a status on social media with a hashtag. The image made her smile, which then reminded her of the fact her cheek was fractured.

"Why was I restrained?" Her wrists looked chafed, but she couldn't imagine she'd tried to hurt anyone.

"With your facial injury we need to keep you elevated as much as possible, and not put any pressure on the already injured area. You kept tapping your face, which is normal for someone who's gone through a traumatic experience such as you. We didn't have to do any reconstructive surgery at this time as the CT scan and X-rays showed your bones stayed in their normal position." He looked at her with a question in his stern expression.

She had no clue what he wanted her to say, tiredness made it hard for her to think clearly. Licking her dry lips, she looked at the cup of water. "May I have another drink?"

He nodded, giving her more.

Once she didn't feel like her mouth was drier than the dirt on a summer day, she finally asked a question that had been burning in her mind. "How long have I been here?"

Looking at his watch, Dr. Davalari's brow furrowed. "Almost eighteen hours. Alright, you need to rest. See this pump." He handed her a cord with a button on the end. "You are in charge of your medication. When you are in pain, you push the button and it'll release your next dosage. Don't worry, you can't give yourself too much. Now, try to rest. We'll get you moved to a regular room shortly."

The tubes in her nose steadily giving her oxygen bothered her. "Can I take this out?"

With a shake of his head, he made a note in the tablet on the cart. "When you've had a facial fracture, even if you don't need surgery, there's a chance your nasal passage could become blocked. We don't want to take the chance that you'll stop breathing while you sleep. Why don't you press that button and get some relief from the pain."

Jaqui hated the thought of closing her eyes again, but the throbbing had become a sharp knife wrenching pulse, beating through her entire being. Her thumb hovered over the top, and then she pushed.

The nurse Molly flittered around, emptying bags and looking at Jaqui like she was a circus freak. The way she was looking, she was probably right. Maybe when she woke up next time she'd ask for a mirror. God, her hair had to be a complete mess. A pixie cut just might be in her future she thought as she finally felt some relief.

"Thank you for taking care of me, Doc."

"No need to thank me, young lady."

She wasn't sure, but Jaqui thought he might have blushed, and even smiled a little. Her eyes became too heavy to keep open. "The rest of my team…are they okay?" God, she hadn't even asked about them.

"I wasn't given any information as it's classified." He looked at the nurse and then back to Jaqui.

Yeah, she was aware, but dammit, she needed to know if Kai and the others were alright.

"Sleep. You can't do anything for anyone but yourself right now, soldier." The gentle reminder gave her the push she needed to let sleep claim her.

****

Tay sat in the seat of the plane, counting the hours since he'd handed Jaqui over. The last they'd heard she had woken only to mumble a few incoherent words, then she would pass out again.

"How the hell could he escape without anyone seeing him?" Sully's unusual green eyes met his across the bay. They were sitting in the C-130 nicknamed Hercules, on their way back to Hawaii, while Jaqui was at Walter Reed.

"It's not right. She's part of our team. Do they have enough security to cover her?" Tay looked at the men he thought of as his brothers.

Kai ran a hand down his face. "Let me see what the Commander says."

They watched in silence as Kai used the satellite phone. The grim expression had his gut tied up in knots. He'd disregard orders and take a commercial flight to Maryland if it came to it. With his mind made up, he sat back and closed his eyes.

Strapped into the seat with the harness around his shoulders and lap, plans formed of how he'd get from Hawaii to Maryland. The extra time would feel like years, but he consoled himself with the knowledge she was in the best place, with military personnel. Surely the Commander wouldn't have left her without a few guards, knowing she would be a target.

"Alright, I got us cleared as Jaqui's security detail. Not that it took too much convincing. I think Lee has knowledge he ain't sharing with me, and that ain't good." Kai took the seat next to Tay.

"What's that mean? You think he's gotten intel the cartel is tracking her?" Tay's hands clenched into fists.

Kai stared straight ahead instead of meeting his eyes. "I'd say that is a high probability. She'll have us

81

on her like stink on shit. No way in hell they'll get their hands on her again."

Tay didn't say what was on his mind, and that she was under their protection the last time they got their hands on her. His friends already blamed themselves.

"For what it's worth, I'm sorry man. None of us thought she was in any danger. Hell, she wasn't even officially part of the team. Her role was research, and wasn't even listed. Fuck, we'd only just left that morning. We weren't even staying in the same location. She was staying at a luxury resort. Have we ever stayed at anything resembling luxury on a mission?" Kai finally turned toward Tay, remorse evident in every facet of his face.

The anger he held washed away. Not the fierce hate and anger at Jose Medellin, but at his team. They'd done exactly what he would've in the same position. Hell, if he'd been cleared, she wouldn't have been his pseudo replacement. Even if she had been on the team while he'd been there, the fact was, it would've played out the same way.

"It's not your fault, Kai. Let's lay the blame where it belongs, and that's with the bastards who took her, and then decided to use her for a punching bag. I only pray she lets me close enough to help her heal inside as well as out." He leaned back on a sigh. Images of her bruised and swollen face, the pitiful sounds of her pain-filled moans would haunt him for the rest of his life.

"Hey, our women are tough. Jaqui will come out kicking ass and taking names," Kai said with conviction.

Kai's woman was one hell of a woman. She'd been beaten within an inch of her life by a crazy ex-boyfriend, then kidnapped by a crazy female. If she could overcome that, and still love Kai without fear, then maybe he and Jaqui had a chance.

The rest of the trip was made in relative silence. Once they landed at the Navy base, each of them cleaned up and changed. Feeling a little more human, they loaded up and headed to the hospital. He was too keyed up for small talk. His friends understood, keeping to themselves what they were all thinking.

None knew if Jaqui had been violated in the worst way a woman could be. Physical injuries a body could heal from. It was the mental ones that only time could take care of, and even then, it wasn't a given. No matter, Tay swore he'd be with her every step of the way.

"You need to put your game face on, man. That look right there will make children run screaming for their mommy and daddy," Coyle said from beside him.

Tay raised his brows. "What the hell are you going on about?"

Coyle made a face. "See that? Did I just look like I was gonna rip your head off and shit down your throat?" He pointed at his own mug before continuing. "Well, that is what you were looking like. You go in the hospital like that, and not only will the hospital staff freak, Jaqui will get upset. You need to go in all chill and shit."

"When did you become an expert on Jaqui?" Tay got in Coyle's face.

"Back the hell off. Coyle's right. None of us need to go in with anger, or pity showing. She'd kick us all out. Least of all you, Tay. You go in and be anything other than the man who she needs, and you could make whatever progress she's done crumble. She's one of us. Hooyah," Kai yelled.

The other guys echoed his yell, but it took Tay a few seconds to pull himself together. In his mind he understood what his friends were saying was true. Hell, Kai had seen firsthand what his woman had gone through. However, all of that was before he'd met her. Taking a deep breath, he let it out.

"I'm sorry, Coyle. I fucked up with Jaqui a while back. If I don't get a chance to make it right with her now...I," he swallowed audibly. "She's the best thing that ever happened to me, and I walked away like a fucking pussy."

Coyle punched him in the arm. "First step is admitting you were wrong and apologizing. Women love that shit."

"Yeah, grovel and beg. They love it when you do that, too. Or so I'm told. Not that I'm ever wrong or anything," Dallas Holt said from the driver's seat. The demolitions expert was filling in for Oz, and had a wicked sense of humor.

They parked the large SUV in the parking garage, exiting the vehicle with caution. Each of them aware the cartel could already be in America. Since they already had Jaqui's room number, they bypassed the information desk, and went straight toward the bank of elevators. The five of them made a few heads turn, but most people there were used to military men and women.

A little boy with a toy train stood with his mother by the elevator, looking up at Kai, the thumb of one hand in his mouth. When the elevator opened the mother stepped in, but the kid hung back, his gaze looking at each of them. Tay wondered if the boy's father was a patient.

"Timmy, come on, baby," the mother said, grabbing the little boys arm.

"Are you GI Joe?" The boy asked Kai.

Coyle laughed.

The woman gasped, trying to tug the kid into the elevator. Seeing her dilemma, Kai and the rest of them moved forward as well, leaving the kid no choice but to enter.

"Nope. GI Joe is in the Army. I'm in the Navy." Kai ruffled the kid's hair.

"Oh. I like the army." The boy turned to his mom and held his hand out for her.

Tay nudged Kai. "I guess we don't measure up, bro," he whispered.

The mom looked embarrassed. "I'm so sorry. He's obsessed with his GI Joe toys. They don't make Navy ones."

"It's okay, really," Kai assured her, giving his patent smile that charmed women over. "My fiancée has said the same thing."

The elevator doors opened on Jaqui's floor. Luckily the woman and kid stayed on, because Tay was pretty sure the woman would've wanted to continue to chat with Kai, while the other man had already dismissed her.

# Chapter Four

Jaqui was going batshit stir crazy in the hospital. She'd been moved to a regular room a little over twenty-four hours ago, but wanted to go home. The beaches of Hawaii would be a much better place to rest and recuperate rather than beige walls, beeping monitors, and doors that opened at all hours of the day and night. Not to mention, having a guard at her door, because they were sure someone from the cartel was going to try to kill her. Yeah, she was ready to go home and have her own things surrounding her. Like her guns and knives.

"That does not look like a face of someone who is happy to see me," Dallas Holt strolled into her room.

She jerked at the sudden deep voice, remembering at the last minute not to smile too big. "Why as I live and breathe, Dallas the snake. What brings you all the way here?" She looked behind the big Texan, amazed to see the rest of the Phantom Team filing in behind.

Her heart squeezed as Taylor Rouland came in last. It had been almost eighteen months since she'd given him her virginity, yet it seemed like yesterday. His blond hair was buzzed on the sides with a little more on top with the bluest eyes she'd ever seen. At thirty-one, he was only four years older than her, but he had seemed so much wiser.

Kai walked up to the bed, his commanding presence undeniable. "What did I tell you about staying out of trouble?" He pulled on the braid she had lying over one shoulder.

"Well, you see, it just wasn't my lucky day. Or rather days I guess. Imagine little ole me, minding my business, enjoying the parade. When all of a sudden I'm surrounded by thugs." She closed her eyes on the memory. The frightening sensation of being powerless as she was in a crowd of people. "They walked right up, one on each side, and then a man stepped in front of me, blocking my view. When I looked up, he bent as if he was going to say something, then placed a cloth over my mouth, but made it look as though we were kissing. I'm not sure what happened after that. I assume I was drugged and carried out. More than likely, to onlookers, I looked like I had too much to drink and my boyfriend had to carry me home." She shrugged although the thought of what they could have done to her still gave her nightmares.

"I figured it was something like that. We've been briefed on your injuries, but wanted you to tell us, if you could, about what went down." Kai's fingers tapped the railing.

Looking at the men surrounding her bed, she looked at their faces. Coyle's hands were behind his back, but he looked her in the eyes. Dallas's teasing grin was missing. Tay stood close to the door staring at his feet, hands fisted at his side. She knew they wondered if she'd been violated. Raped. Lord, how she hated that thought herself.

"I woke up in a concrete room on a dirty floor, fully clothed, guys. I was starved for days, then when I did eat, I got sick. I was beaten, yes. I was drugged and beat some more, but I was not raped. Promise. The last day...I think would have been a different story, but the compound I was being held in was attacked. I'd been released from my holding cell to shower and while there a gunfight happened. I stayed hidden and when I came out, I saw my chance to escape and did." She explained her run through the forest.

"Tay carried you up while we radioed for a Helivac. You scared the shit right out of us, woman." Kai glared at her, warmth lit his dark eyes.

She tried to make sense of his words. "You guys found me?" Her eyes searched out Tay standing by the door still. Finally he looked up, meeting her gaze.

Kai cleared his throat. "Well, we couldn't let you just lie around all damn day."

She covered his big hand with hers. "Alexa is a lucky woman. Thank you for carrying me out of there, Taylor," she said without looking directly at him again.

Soft footfalls squeaked across the floor. "I was a damn fool. My heart nearly stopped when I saw you lying beneath that jaguar. For that moment in time, I swore to God that I wouldn't make the same mistake again, and here I am standing by the door like a jackhole." He paused and looked at Kai. "Could you guys give us a minute?"

"Sure thing. We'll run down to the coffee shop. I could use some liquid gold right about now." He bent and placed a chaste kiss on Jaqui's forehead. "Go easy on him. We menfolk tend to be idiots when it comes to matters of the heart."

Coyle patted her leg. "Not me. I'm smarter than the average guy. See you in a bit. Give him hell."

Tay flipped him the bird.

"I, for one, happen to be a total ladies man. I know just what they want, and how to give it to them," Dallas said wickedly.

Kai punched him in the arm "Which is why you're single. Let's go before I throw up in my mouth."

The three of them continued to argue as they walked out. Tension mounted as the door shut and she waited for Tay to say something.

"I'm sorry for so much, Jaqui." He came closer, voice dropping.

A lump formed in her throat. "Thank you for saying that."

He paced away, hands behind his back. "You see, when I realized how innocent you were, I freaked. My plan wasn't to settle down just yet." He looked at her over his shoulder. "Then this pint sized, gorgeous woman with hair down to her ass, blew me away from the first moment I saw her. At first I thought we could date. You know be casual. Again, you knocked me off my axis."

Unsure what he wanted her to say, she sat, pleating the blanket between her fingers.

"You got a text while you were sleeping. I wasn't snooping or anything, but worried it was important, so I went to retrieve your phone, and the message was lit up." He met her stare before continuing. "Seeing your friend's words about getting an invite to the wedding, it scared me."

She knew what he was talking about and could imagine the shock he probably felt at seeing the text.

Hell, any guy would have felt the same. Maybe. "You do realize she was joking. I didn't expect you to propose just because we'd had sex." It had been much more than that for her.

He crossed the room in three angry strides. "Don't pretend like it was just sex. You and I both know it was much more. I felt it, you felt it so don't deny it or us. I'd kiss you right now and show you, but I don't want to hurt you. Damn it. I should have stayed." He closed his eyes as if in pain.

"Even if you had…you know stayed, this would have happened. I mean we don't know what would or wouldn't have. Don't blame yourself for what that monster did to me. I'll heal and be back on my feet in no time." She tried to inflict as much confidence in her tone as possible.

One big palm lifted, then touched her cheek. The feather light touch made her breath catch. She closed her eyes and leaned into his touch. "I'd do anything to take the pain away if I could."

"I'm just glad it's over." A tightening in his muscled forearm had her opening her eyes to look up at him. "What is it?"

Tay shook his head. "It's nothing for you to worry about."

When he would have moved his hand away, she grabbed it. "If this has anything to do with Medellin, then I do. I've seen old pictures of him, and I can tell y'all right now, he has had some cosmetic changes. That man is pure evil. He showed no emotion as he hit me. When he ordered his men to do things, his tone was completely devoid of emotion. But, his eyes held what I'd call anticipation. Like he enjoyed what they were going to do."

"You realize he got away? Even now he could have men or women in this hospital, right? Until he's either caught or dead you won't be safe," he growled.

She shrugged, the motion pulled at aches in her body. "What am I supposed to do, Tay? Go into hiding? Commander Lee hasn't mentioned anything to me about what happens next. All I know is my injuries aren't life threatening, and I'm pretty sure

I'm being released today or tomorrow. It's not like I can't protect myself." Well, in normal circumstances she could. She hadn't been prepared to be kidnapped in the middle of a crowd and neither had the rest of the team. Security in numbers clearly wasn't true in all situations.

"Sure you can. I mean look at you." He waved his hand over her prone form. "Can you even make a fist?"

Jaqui raised her right hand and lifted her middle finger. "Oh yeah, big guy. Listen, all this will take time, but not forever. In a few days, most of it will be nothing more than a memory." A freaking nightmare, but he didn't need to know that.

"Sure, cupcake, and I'm the tooth fairy if you believe that shit you're spouting."

She grinned, then winced. "I can totally see you in a pink tutu with a sparkly wand. I'd ask you to sprinkle some glitter on me to make me look less garish."

He came back over to the bed, lowering the railing to sit next to her hip. Bending down so his face

97

was in front of hers, he brushed his lips over every bruise and cut on her, starting on her forehead and working down to her chin. "You are the most beautiful woman I have ever seen. Even with all this, you are gorgeous. I'd give my left arm to have prevented you from any injury. If I could take back the things I've said and done, I'd do it. Everything except that day in the hotel with you, right up to me leaving. I'm a dumbass. That can't be denied," he laughed. "Let me make it up to you by taking care of you while you recover. We can start fresh. Like dating, since we sort of skipped that."

It was hard for her to think with him sitting so close. They'd gone out for a couple months back before that night, but he must not have considered that dating. His clear blue eyes promised things she wanted to believe. The gentle touch of his kisses had her leaning into his warmth. "What about your mission? The Phantom Team? Aren't you guys still supposed to be searching for Medellin?"

Tay's thumb brushed over her bottom lip. Her tongue peeked out, tasting him. "My mission is to protect you. Our team's mission is to protect each other."

She opened her mouth to ask more, but a knock on the door stopped her. She expected Tay to get up and act like the aloof SEAL. He surprised her again as he sat, uncaring who entered and saw him.

Commander Lee strode in. His larger than life presence intimidating as always. Tay stood and saluted. "Sir," he said.

"Rouland, glad to see your team all made it out of Columbia. Wallace, girl, you sure do know how to get into the thick of things." Shrewd gray eyes assessed her.

"Yes, sir, Commander Lee. I've been debriefed and given my official statement. I should be ready for active duty in a couple weeks."

The Commander shook his head. "As of right now, you are on medical leave. The Phantom Team are officially assigned to you. This is a serious situation that we are not taking lightly."

He went on to explain her travel plans. Not once giving her a chance to speak, which was good. Jaqui didn't look at Tay during the entire ten minutes the Commander was issuing his orders, knowing he would not like to have had his life rearranged because of her. Yes, he'd said he wanted to take care of her, but to have his choices taken away had to chafe.

"Any questions?" Commander Lee looked at her, then Tay.

"No, Commander Lee. Thank you for coming yourself."

Commander Lee waved his hand. "I was in Washington on official business. I've already spoken to your leader out in the hall, and believe he has everything in hand in regards to the travel. I'll just leave it at that. Before you ask, we've already sent another team after Medellin, but that doesn't mean you need to relax your guard. Our intel says he's in the Middle East, but that doesn't mean crap today."

Tay nodded, while she felt like her world was spinning out of control.

"Alright, I must go." He checked his watch, then after a few more words left.

"I'm sorry, Tay. I didn't mean to upset you and the guys' lives like this." Knowing how much the SEALs enjoyed their missions, she hated to be the cause of them being stuck on land.

A laugh burst from Tay. "Are you kidding? Alexa will probably buy you flowers or something since having Kai home on a mission will be a change of pace. Besides, do you not remember what I was saying before the Commander had come in?" He sat back down carefully.

She sighed. "I promise not to be a pain in the ass."

He picked up her braid. "You could never be that."

"You have no clue. I'm considered a real bear in the mornings if I don't get my coffee. I mean, do not talk to me until after the first cup. I also take forever in the shower, so be prepared to wait your turn."

Heat lit his eyes. "Not if we share one."

Her stomach flipped at the thought. "Taylor Rouland, I do declare, you are a naughty boy."

"You've no clue, baby."

****

If he could've kissed Commander Lee for giving him the perfect excuse to spend twenty-four seven with Jaqui he would've. Of course, having the rest of the team there wasn't in his original plans, but with the threat of not just Medellin, but the cartel looming over Jaqui, he welcomed the extra security.

He saw the arousal his words brought light her bruised and battered face, and wished he could act on it, vowing he'd make it up to Jaqui soon. "When you are well enough, I'll show you just how much fun it can be to share a shower with me. I have this fantasy about washing your hair."

"I seriously think you are crazy. It takes forever to wash and get all the shampoo out, not to mention conditioning all this. I was thinking while I was…in the room they held me in, that I should just cut it all off," she whispered.

Tipping her chin up with his finger, he held her stare. "I love your hair. I'd spend hours if that's what it took. However, it you wanted to cut it, because that is what *you* want, I would totally understand. But don't let that bastard dictate what you do. Don't give him any more power."

Her lip trembled. "I was so scared."

Careful of her bruises, and the IVs, he gathered her into his arms. For the first time in over a year, he felt like he'd finally come home. Sitting in a hospital, holding Jaqui Wallace, he finally felt complete.

Another knock on the door interrupted them. He didn't want to pull away. With reluctance he eased her back down, wiped the tears from beneath her eyes, then stood back up. "Enter," he barked.

"Damn, boy. Why you growling like I kicked your puppy?" Dallas asked, coming in with a cup of coffee in each hand. He took one look at Jaqui, then his head jerked over to Tay. "What the hell happened?"

"We are her official team of guards," Tay said, he glared at Dallas.

"Cool. Here, brought you a coffee." Dallas held out his arm.

Tay looked over to see what Jaqui thought, but she was looking at the door and the rest of the guys filing in. God love her, she had no clue they would all take a bullet for her.

Kai filled them in on the travel plans for the next day, unless the doctor doesn't release Jaqui. "I've spoken to Alexa. She's excited to see you again, so I hope you are up for a little female company when we get home."

Jaqui looked to him before answering. "I'd like to see her, too."

"Good to hear. I'm afraid she's a bit of a bulldozer. If you'd have said anything else, she'd have orchestrated a get together." His eyes lit up with admiration that Tay understood. The woman who'd captured the big SEAL's heart had been through hell and back, yet she still had a heart of gold. Having been in the foster care system her entire life until she'd aged out, Alexa had thought her parents had been killed. It wasn't until a crazy ex-boyfriend, had almost beaten her to death that she hit the system as alive, waking up a network of international spies who had been looking for her, and her parents. Luckily for her, or unluckily, when she went on the run after the near death experience, she'd been kidnapped. Kai and the rest of their team were the ones who'd saved her, and the rest as they say was history. Now, Alexa and her parents were reunited and she had made it her mission to find all the men their own women.

"I think she and I will get along just fine," she assured Kai.

"Alright, we need to get a couple rooms for the night. Tay, you staying here or what?" Kai didn't sound surprised, which Tay should've known the other man knew how he felt.

"If they'll let me, yeah."

Coyle barked out a laugh. "Pretty sure they won't be able to stop your ass. Besides, you're on official duty and shit."

Dallas raised his hand. "I volunteer to speak to the nurse on duty."

Tay looked at the men, his brothers, and waited.

Coyle's hands moved in a motion that let him know the woman was clearly stacked. Shaking his head, he turned to Jaqui. "You okay with this?" he whispered.

Her cheeks were red, but she nodded.

Dallas walked out of the room, presumably to ask, or flirt with the nurse about getting Tay a bed. For all Tay cared, he'd sleep standing up for the next twenty-four hours.

"Is there still going to be a guard outside the door?" He asked Kai.

"Yeah. Until she's discharged there will be one posted." Kai stood at the end of the bed. I've read your statement. Is there anything you didn't include, or something that you've remembered since then?"

Tay went to stand next to the bed, his hand automatically reaching for hers.

She shook her head. "No. Like I said in my statement. I woke up in a room with concrete walls. There was a drain in the middle. I only left the one time when they decided to take me to see Medellin. I guess I was too smelly for his taste. While I was showering, with my clothes on, we heard the gunshots. My jailer left me in there, but didn't lock the door. I hid until I didn't hear anymore, then made my way back." They listened as she explained how she found the guard dead outside the door to Medellin's office and made a mental note of the man's name, then her escape through the rainforest. Her hand releasing his to wipe on the blanket.

He had to grip the railing and noticed his knuckles had turned white from where he'd clenched them. In his mind he could imagine the horror she'd experienced. How she must have felt thinking at any minute they could come in and do anything they wanted to her. The images in his mind had him shaking. One pale, slim hand with IV's taped to it rested on top of his, making him unclench his.

"You need to stop that or you're going to bend the metal." Her tone was teasing, yet he didn't feel like smiling. When they'd arrived at the cinder block building, he had no clue what they'd find. The thought of being too late had made sweat and nausea roll over him in waves. As they'd entered the compound and walked over bodies, his gaze swept from side to side looking for blonde hair, and hoping not to find her, yet wishing she was there.

"Yo, earth to Tay." Kai snapped his fingers across Jaqui's bed.

"What did you say?" He looked around, clearing the images of blood and death from his mind.

"I said, we were gonna head out and get rooms for the night. You want us to bring you back something to eat?"

Tay looked down at the sleepy looking woman. "No, I'll just see if I can't get whatever she's having."

Jaqui snorted. "So far I've had broth, juice and water. I think you'll starve, big guy."

"Don't worry about me. There's a cafeteria I can get something from."

Kai gave him an assessing glance, then pecked Jaqui on the cheek. "You stay out of trouble, and don't let this one do anything stupid. We'll be back in the morning."

He had to stand by while the rest of the team said their goodbyes, even Dallas, who being the clown he was tried to kiss her on the lips, but failed as she turned her cheek with a laugh.

"You know I would rip your lips off, Dallas. Besides, who knows where those things have been." She gave a mock shudder.

Dallas frowned. "Hey, I haven't had them anywhere." He paused. "Lately." Winking, he sauntered out ahead of the others.

"That boy is gonna get in more trouble with some lady, or because of a lady," Kai said, waving as he walked out the door.

"I didn't think they'd ever leave. How are you feeling?" Tay sat back in the spot by her hip. He could see she was trying to hide the fact she was hurting from him.

"They took the pain pump out this morning when they moved me up here. I'm not sure when I'm due for meds." Looking at the clock with a forlorn expression, she grimaced.

Tay knew what he'd gone through, and pushed the call button, explaining what they wanted to the voice over the speaker, he stayed next to Jaqui even when the nurse came in. He looked at the woman's name, and watched as she gave the dose.

"Can I place an order for dinner along with Jaqui, or do I need to go down to the cafeteria myself, Heather?" He knew the answer, but wanted to see how the lady would answer.

"You can order a meal, and as luck would have it, Ms. Wallace is cleared for a regular diet as well. I'll bring you both back a menu. Now, don't get excited, it's not the best selection, but better than broth," she laughed then walked out.

Jaqui patted his hand. "You can stop planning all the ways she can be killed now."

The slurred tone of her voice had him looking down. He loved that she understood just what he was thinking, and was fine with it. Many women would have been appalled at his thoughts, but his Jaqui made a joke, and accepted it and him. Loved. Yeah, he was pretty sure he loved her. Like head over ass loved. Watching her eyes drift shut, he promised to always keep her safe, even if it meant he had to kick his own ass.

He tensed as the door opened, holding his finger to his mouth, he eased up from the bed and met the nurse halfway across the room. Quickly he scanned the card and ordered for both he and Jaqui. She looked over to the bed and the sleeping Jaqui, then smiled and nodded.

"I'll place the order now," she said quietly.

"Thanks, I appreciate it."

After checking that he didn't need anything else, she left. Tay wanted to lay next to Jaqui and hold her, but worried he'd wake her up, and didn't want to cause eyebrows to raise at Walter Reed. Instead, he pulled the reclining chair next to the bed and sat.

The cell in his pocket vibrated. Pulling it out, he read a text from Kai, letting him know where they were staying. He told him all was good, and that he had dinner handled. Before he replaced his phone, he opened his browser and checked to see if there was any news about the drug cartels. Although the government liked to keep missions hush hush, sometimes the media caught wind of things, which was not good for those in the military. His search came up with nothing, making him relax. Opening his email, he scrolled through, deleted several until he came to one from his mom. The woman was tenacious in her quest to get him married so she could have grandbabies. His head jerked up, automatically looking at Jaqui. His mother would love the petite blonde. Of course, she'd nag Jaqui about giving up her career, which would not be good. He shook his head as he thought of things that hadn't even transpired. "Moving way ahead of yourself boyo."

He let his mom know he was back on U.S. soil and would be heading home to Hawaii the next day, promising to call once he was settled. Since the woman didn't check her email daily, he wasn't sure when she'd actually see it, he figured he had a little reprieve.

Sitting back, he placed his folded hands over his stomach. With time to kill, he let his eyes close. Rest had been the last thing on his mind since finding out Jaqui had been taken. Now, he let his body relax, his mind following. The slow steady beeping lulled him into sleep.

Two things alerted him to the fact they were no longer alone. The first was when he heard the door open softly. The second was the sound of the soft soled shoes tiptoeing across the floor. Tay kept his breathing slow and easy, waiting to see what the intruder would do, and wondering where the guard on duty was. He hoped he didn't have to kill anyone while in the military hospital, but he'd do what he had to. Mind made up, he opened his eyes to slits, watching as the nurse from earlier looked around Jaqui. He saw her lift something out of her pocket, then glance in his direction, a slight frown marring her forehead. Her right hand fisted, she lifted one of the IV's attached to Jaqui.

"Whatcha got there, nurse?" Tay opened his eyes, keeping his voice even.

The woman sputtered, dropping what she had in her hand on the ground. Tay sprang into action as she tried to flee from the room. "Where you going? Shouldn't you be picking up that there medicine, and doing what you came here for? Or were you thinking you could run fast enough? Let me save you some time and energy," he growled, getting in her face. "There ain't nowhere you can run or hide from me that would keep you safe. Had you succeeded in your mission, you'd be the one lying in a cold, hard grave." With each word his voice raised until he was sure nobody on the floor could fail to hear him. The sound of pounding feet let him know others were coming in. Whether it was to save him and Jaqui or the nurse, was yet to be seen. He held onto the nurse with one arm, while he bent down and retrieved the injection with the other.

"I'm sorry. I had to do it. They told me if I didn't they'd kill my baby. If I don't report back with it being done, my son will be killed." The woman sobbed.

He looked in her eyes, but didn't see true tears. He'd thought something was off with the woman earlier.

Fishing into his pocket, he dialed Kai. Within one ring the other man answered. "Kai, I need you to find out if Heather Angelique is a nurse here at Walter Reed, and if so, if she has a son." He listened to Kai, then continued. "Yeah, she just tried to kill Jaqui."

The officer who was stationed outside the door walked in to hear the last part, his eyes flying open, gun coming out of its holster. A shiver wracked the woman's frame, but she didn't say another word. Either her cover was good, or she didn't care what happened to herself.

"I'm sorry, sir. There was supposedly an incident at the elevators. She asked me to help a mother with an injured child, but when I got there," he looked down at his toes, then up. "There was no one there. I foolishly thought the mother had found her child and had just started back when I heard your raised voice. I've alerted the hospital that we are on lockdown. Should I..." his voice trailed off.

Tay stared at the young soldier. "Yeah, lift it, and don't ever leave your post again. If there is ever a situation, you call for backup. Period. You are on duty, soldier. You don't abandon your post. Understand me?"

"What's going on, Tay?" Jaqui questioned.

# Chapter Five

Jaqui eyed the nurse from earlier, seeing her rigid posture as she was held by Tay's grip on her upper bicep, and his uncompromising glare gave her pause. The woman turned to stare at her over her shoulder, the anger that burned in the blue eyes stunned Jaqui.

"Looks like I missed some action." She gave the woman a glare of her own.

"This traitor tried to inject something into your IV while you and I were sleeping. Luckily, I'm a light sleeper." Tay gave the woman a little shake.

The guard stood with a look of despair. "I apologize for leaving my post. What do you want me to do with her?" He nodded at the nurse named Heather.

Tay looked around the room, then his eyes landed on the soldier. "What do you have to hold a prisoner? Cuffs, zip ties, anything like that?"

The guard nodded his head, then fished in his pocket for the zip ties. Heather tried to jerk free. "If you'd like I can render you unconscious." Tay said loud enough for them all to hear.

"Make sure you don't do like last time, hun. We want her to be able to talk again, not be a slobbering fool for the rest of her natural life," Jaqui said with false sweetness.

Heather's posture changed, her head whipped toward Jaqui's. "What? I thought you guys were the honorable ones?"

Jaqui stretched her hand toward the water cup, then pulled it back, a question in her eyes. "That's only true in the case of the good and worthy. You, my dear, are none of the above."

"I'll get you a new glass. Don't drink or touch anything she may have contaminated." Tay finished tying the woman up.

Tay's phone buzzed.

Jaqui sat, her body tense while she waited for Kai's answers. "Thank you. Yeah, I'd say our location is compromised." They spoke a few more minutes, while Heather sat in a chair with the guard behind her.

"Commander Lee is sending someone to take out the trash, and we are moving you to a secure location. You obviously know your story didn't check out. Good try though, it would have passed most checks, but Kai has my computer with him."

She'd wondered why he hadn't brought it with him. The man, like herself was hardly ever without their links to the internet. Right now she was too tired to think clearly long enough. Give her another day, and she would need her connection.

"It does not matter. When I don't check in, Jose will know you are not dead, and will move on to his next plan. You should have let me kill her. Now, you and your friends will all suffer," Heather's natural Spanish accent broke free.

Tay tsked, then looked at the guard. "I need you to go to the vending machine and get Jaqui a bottle of water. Don't open it and make it fast."

The guy stood straight, saluted and rushed from the room.

"You realize Medellin doesn't allow those who fail him to live, don't you?" Tay asked, his voice dropping low.

Heather turned her head toward the window, but Jaqui knew the other woman was aware Tay spoke the truth.

The door opened at the same time as Tay's phone rang. "Watch her, and don't let her up." He pointed at Heather, and walked closer to the door.

"You should have died in Columbia. Now, I will pay for your stupidity," Heather spat.

"What a dumb bitch you are. What do you get out of this?" Jaqui waved her hand around the room. "Other than killing me, do you know what Medellin does? He sells drugs and people. I'm not wasting another breath on the likes of you." She sat back with a weary sigh.

Tay strolled back over. "Your escort is on their way up."

"I'll get a phone call, right?" Fear finally registered.

"This isn't like the movies," Tay drawled.

With the bottle of water in his hand, Tay came to stand next to her, opening it plopping a new straw inside. "Sorry, I got distracted."

Instead of answering, she wrapped her lips around the end and drank. Lord, she was thirsty enough she felt like she could drink the entire bottle. Looking up, she met the amused stare of Tay's, and let the straw go. "I was a little thirsty."

He laughed. "I can see that." He put his lips close to her ear. "Damn, but watching you, even with two people in the room, with your lips wrapped around that straw, has me half hard. Now, how's that for crazy?"

She knew her face had to be bright red. "I'd say it's normal for the situation," she whispered back.

Tay ran a big hand over her head, careful of her injuries. "We'll be out of here in no time."

No time ended up being just before the shift changed the next morning. Jaqui wasn't sure what she'd expected, but having her IV's taken out by Coyle wasn't one of them, although the big guy was truly gentle. Of course, with Tay standing over her like a mother hen, he had no choice. They wheeled her out through the staff exit, to a waiting Hummer. She assumed it was military grade on steroids as it didn't look like one she'd ever seen before.

"This is on loan from a friend of mine. If something tries to blow this bad boy up, we will survive, trust and believe that," Kai said with a wink.

The soft leather was much better than what the military provided as well, but still, the move wasn't pleasant on her sore body. Tay squeezed in next to her on one side with Dallas on the other. Kai and Coyle sat up front.

"Here, take one of these now." Tay handed her a pill.

She shook her head. "I don't want to be a liability if something went wrong."

Coyle turned in the seat. "Sweetheart, I hate to break it to you, but seeing you sit there in pain, hurts us. We would all relax just a bit, and you'd make it just that much easier on us if you took the drugs. Seriously, you are hurting the team by refusing Tay."

Tay held the little pill and a can of ginger ale. She'd gotten very little sleep the night before, knowing there was a mark on her head. After eating a small breakfast, they'd immediately left. Now, she reached for the pill and the drink, swallowing it down with a grimace.

"Fine, but if I pass out, it's up to you guys to carry my ass around." She gave them a mock glare.

Coyle turned back around, but not before she saw him smile.

"I'll gladly carry you around, sweets." Tay lifted her hand into his.

Their linked hands didn't raise any of the guys' eyebrows, which made her wonder how much they knew about her and Tay's past.

"They only know I fucked up. Nothing more. Nothing less," Tay leaned close, his warm breath sent a shiver down her body.

"I didn't say anything." She turned to look him in the eye.

He brought their linked hands up to his mouth, pressing a kiss to her knuckles. "You didn't have to. You have very expressive eyes."

"Where are we heading?" She turned to look at the road.

"Home," Kai said from the front.

"Is that smart?" She'd love to go home, but worried about bringing trouble to their front doors.

\*\*\*\*

Tay didn't intend to allow her to go home alone. No, he would be with her twenty-four seven. They had a plan, and when a SEAL had a plan, all would be fine. Failure was not an option, and in this case it most definitely was not. They'd almost lost Jaqui once, he'd be damned if it happened again.

"Quit frowning, it'll cause premature wrinkles." Jaqui rubbed her thumb between his brows.

He could see the slight action caused her some discomfort. "Try not to move too much." He lifted her hand onto his thigh, hating the bruises on the top from where the IVs had been. Tracing his finger along the bluish lines, he promised to do all he could to never see the same marring her beautiful skin again. "I hate seeing you hurt."

"Almost at the hangar, then we'll be in the air and home before you know it," Kai said from the front.

Flying from the East Coast to Hawaii was a long flight, no matter how they traveled. Stopping in California so their plane could refuel, they stayed on board while Dallas and Coyle went to get them all something to eat.

He eased out of the chair, making sure Jaqui slept. "What aren't you telling us?" Tay asked Kai once he reached the front of the aircraft.

"I don't think Medellin, or the Bloque Cartel for that matter, are happy with us. They will be out for blood. With the one tie they can connect being that little gal back there. The leader isn't known for

125

losing, and to have a woman escape would be the ultimate insult to him." Kai's dark gaze stared back toward Jaqui's sleeping form.

Tay felt the force of the implication hit him. "How the fuck does he know she wasn't killed in that attack, Kai?" He'd realized they'd had a leak when the woman who'd been pretending to be a nurse had tried to kill Jaqui. Now he wondered if their location was compromised as well.

Kai stood taller in the galley of the plane. "That's what I aim to find out. Which is why we are all going to be staying in the same place for the next few weeks. Call it a mini vacation or staycation, since we'll be on our home turf. Nobody will be allowed in or out that we don't trust explicitly, and that number just dropped dramatically."

He searched Kai's expression, and knew the SEAL was talking, not the man. "What about Alexa? I know you want to get back to her."

A grin kicked up the corner of his lips. "Hell yeah I do. She'll be one of the trusted few. Besides, I think Jaqui could use some female company. Don't you?"

What he wanted was time alone with the little spitfire, but until she was healed, it was probably best they had a chaperone. Not that he thought she'd welcome him back into her arms so easily. He'd screwed up and had a lot of making up to do.

"You look like your plotting," Kai muttered, but before he could question further, Coyle and Dallas boarded the plane with their arms full with bags of food.

"What did you do? Buy one of everything you passed?" Kai grabbed a bag from each of them.

Coyle shrugged. "Wasn't sure what you'd want since we weren't sure what was available. Besides, some might taste like cardboard."

Within another half hour their flight was taking off for the final leg of their journey. He'd eaten, then when Jaqui woke gave her some soup the guys had been thoughtful enough to buy.

When they landed at the airstrip at Barking Sands Missile Range Navy Base in Kekaha, Hawaii, they were all ready to find their own beds. With most of them living near base in the plantation style homes at Barking Sands, their bodies seemed to know they were close to home.

It was dark outside as they disembarked the plane, each of them had grabbed a duffel from the overhead compartment before they'd stepped down. Two vehicles sat waiting for them, making Tay raise his eyebrow in question.

"We're not taking any chances. Just roll with it." Kai pointed to the first Hummer.

Tay and Jaqui walked side-by-side to the vehicle Kai indicated. He helped her into the back, noticing the flash of pain race across her bruised and swollen face she tried to hide.

Coyle and Dallas followed behind in the other military vehicle, but nobody said a word, other than the driver to welcome them home. Tay shook his head at the awe in the young soldier's tone as he looked at Kai sitting next to him. Poor kid, Kai didn't seem to notice as he was busy typing on his cell, more than likely letting Alexa know he'd landed and would be there shortly.

He sat back with a sigh, then hoped he'd not left a mess in his own quarters before he'd been called out on his last mission.

Jaqui cleared her throat. "How many bedrooms does Kai's place have?"

Her abrupt question had him turning to stare at her through the dark interior. "Why?"

"Where is everyone staying? I mean I assumed he'd be heading straight home, and said we would all be under the same roof..." her voice trailed off.

"You and I will be staying with Kai and Alexa. Coyle and Oz live a mile or so down, but still not close enough. My cottage is further down, so too far away for safety sake if the need arose. We are the only ones who are in residence on that stretch. Kai has a three bedroom cottage." He didn't tell her that Coyle and Dallas would be sharing one room, while he'd be staying with her. She'd learn soon enough. She was in no shape for anything other than a light brushing of his fingers against most of her body, let alone making love.

She nodded like she'd come up with a plan. God love her and her brain. He'd outmaneuver her of course, but he'd like to see what she devised.

Their escorts pulled up to Kai's home, the house sat up on two foot piers with all the lights in the house blazing. A figure stood at the front door. One Tay knew had been watching ever since Kai's text.

The vehicle hadn't come to a complete stop before Kai had his door open and was leaping down, his long strides eating up the distance between him and the woman now running down the porch steps. Tay heard Jaqui's sigh, felt her pulse beat against his fingers. He wondered if she'd be waiting for him like Alexa when he came home from a mission. Turning his head away as Kai and Alexa embraced, feeling like he was intruding on their moment, his eyes met Jaqui's.

"They're truly in love," she said. It wasn't a question but a statement.

"That man is so in love with her, I can't believe he hasn't married her yet." He opened his door, held his hand out for the woman who held his heart.

He felt Coyle and Dallas at his back, knowing the other guys were ready to protect Jaqui the same as him gave him a sense of ease.

"You coming in or gonna stand out there all night?" Kai called from the bottom of the steps to his home.

Jaqui looked past him, then gave a slight smile. He knew she would have waved broadly, but with her injuries, the action was close to impossible. "We better head on up, but I'm going to need some more of my things." She looked pointedly at his duffle and her lack of one.

"We'll take care of it tomorrow." Jaqui wasn't stationed on the same base as he and his team, but it wouldn't be anything to get someone to pack up a few things for her.

"Hiya, Jaqui. I'm Alexa. We met back in South Dakota," Alexa said, her arm firmly around Kai's waist.

"Ma'am." Jaqui nodded. "Thank you for letting me bunk with you for a few days."

Amethyst eyes blinked out at them. The curvy woman who'd claimed Kai Swift's heart released her SEAL, and stepped forward. "Now, let's clear something up real quick. I'm no ma'am, and you are family. I made a ham and scalloped potatoes knowing y'all would be hungry when you landed, so let's get inside and get you settled. If you'd rather shower and go to bed, that's fine, too. However, what's not fine is this formal shit." Alexa Gordon smiled at them.

Tay could kiss the woman for immediately putting Jaqui at ease. "I could eat."

The other guys said the same.

"I would love some scalloped potatoes. Not sure I can chew the ham, dang it." Jaqui followed Alexa up the few steps to the cottage style house, while he hung back knowing Kai wanted to speak to them.

The screen door shut on a quiet thud. "Alright, let's hear it." Tay waited, his ears trained to the house.

"Alexa is excited to have company. I've told her briefly about the trouble we could be expecting, but as she pointed out, her family and troubles were no Robinsons. Meaning she is not worried. Hence, I am worried." Kai ran his hand over his stubbled chin.

Having not shaved himself, Tay figured he looked pretty gruff as well. "We'll protect them from themselves as well as the shit storm that could be coming."

Coyle slapped him on the back. "Hooyah. Now, didn't I hear something about baked ham and potatoes? Move boys, I'm a starving man."

Kai and Tay were nudged aside as Coyle, followed by Dallas took the steps two at a time.

"You'd think they were kids instead of grown men," Kai muttered.

"Growing boys," Coyle yelled back.

"We'd better hurry or those asshats will eat you out of house and home." Tay motioned with his hand for Kai to go ahead of him.

Inside they were met by Oz, his red hair a little longer than before. His large frame not looking any thinner from his stay in the hospital.

"Hey, I left y'all some. You're welcome by the way." Oz patted his flat stomach, his eyes taking in their appearances. "How was your trip?"

"Uneventful for the most part." Kai sat down, snagging Alexa when she went to walk by. "Sit down, luv. They can serve themselves. I need to hold you for a few."

The two didn't seem to mind the fact they were surrounded by SEALs. Kai's face buried in the crook of Alexa's neck, making her giggle.

"Get a room," Oz groaned.

Kai's middle finger lifted. "Oh, I plan to take her there. We're just being polite right now."

Alexa slapped Kai's arm, but didn't get up from his lap. Her arms were wrapped around his neck while he forked up pieces of ham and potatoes, feeding himself then her. Tay envied their easy show of affection in that moment. Meeting Jaqui's gaze next to him, he saw the same naked need in her.

"We put you two in the room across from Alexa and I. Coyle and Dallas are next to you and Oz, I'm assuming you're bunking in the living room?" Kai punctuated each word with his fork.

Oz nodded. "Yep."

He noticed Jaqui had eaten a good portion of the food, but was pushing the remaining around. "If you don't mind, I'm going to show Jaqui where we're bunking." Standing, he waited for her to say goodnight.

"You don't have to go to bed because I am." She yawned, her hand going up to cover the area.

Tay didn't say a word, just walked with Jaqui. Opening the door, he wasn't surprised to find Alexa had stacked a few outfits on the end of the bed with a note. Luckily the ladies were close to the same size, although Alexa was a bit curvier. Tay loved Jaqui's physique.

Truth be told, there was nothing about the woman he didn't enjoy. From her long blonde hair, to her sparkling blue eyes, all the way down to her toes. She was perfect for him. He'd seen her training, had the pleasure of seeing her naked, and knew there wasn't an ounce of fat on her frame. Yet, she had muscles. Not the overly done kind that made you think manly, but enough that she could probably lift her own weight and then some. Again, the word perfect rang in his head.

"How that woman survived in foster care is a miracle." He heard the catch in her voice.

Strolling into the room, he checked out the attached bathroom. It was small but had a nice sized shower. Big enough for two. Slow your roll soldier. He checked the window next to the vanity, making sure it was locked. Even knowing Alexa and Kai, he felt better going through the security of the rooms he and Jaqui would be sleeping in. As he walked back out to the bedroom with the queen sized bed, Jaqui sat on the edge, the clothing no longer on the end. A slight frown pulled at her face.

He knelt at her feet. "What's wrong?"

She blinked baby blue eyes up at him. "How is this supposed to work?"

"You are going to rest, heal, and then we reassess. That's what is going to happen," he said with conviction.

"No. I mean you and me. Where are you sleeping?"

It took him a moment, but he considered himself a smart man. "Baby, I am sleeping in this room with you. Maybe not in this bed, but where you are, I am. Believe me, I've slept in a lot less comfy spots than the floor." Her safety was his number one concern.

Leaning up, he placed a kiss on her lips, a whisper soft touch. "How about you go take a quick shower while I check in with Kai and the rest of the team." He didn't give her a chance to argue, wasn't sure she would, but stood and left just in case.

# Chapter Six

Tay walked back down the hallway toward the kitchen. Kai and Alexa were still sitting at the table. The couple looked as if they'd been together years rather than months. A natural extension of each other.

"How's Jaqui doing?" Alexa asked without getting up.

He shrugged. "Pretty good all things considered."

"You want a beer?" Kai asked.

"That sounds about the best damn thing in the world." Tay opened the fridge and grabbed a longneck, looking over the top of the door he glanced at each of the people gathered around, silently asking if they needed one. Coyle raised his empty bottle along with Oz. Dallas shook his head, his phone seemed to be buzzing as if dozens of texts were coming in.

After handing over a beer to each of the men who were more like brothers, he sat down. "Thank you for the clothes. Jaqui mentioning the fact she needed to get some of her own things." He tipped the bottle up to his lips and took a long pull.

Kai shook his head. "I don't think it's safe right now. Her best bet is to keep out of sight. We can get her a cell so she can contact her family, but again, it could be tricky since they could have their phones tapped."

Tay knew he could work around most systems and do the same thing. The U.S. government didn't do such things to civilians, yet a drug cartel, especially one as dirty as the Bloque, who dealt in human and drug trafficking wouldn't think twice about tapping a phone line. More than likely they already had those closest to Jaqui in their sights. Jose Medellin didn't like to lose, even if it was just an American, but especially if it was someone he felt he could use.

"I can get around anything they might have on the lines if I find something. I'll just need my computer and a few other things from my place." Tiredness swept over him.

"Take your ass to bed, or the floor. You can't do anything tonight. We all need sleep. Tomorrow we'll make plans."

Alexa groaned. "You and your plans."

Kai stood, tossing Alexa over his shoulder. "I think you'll like some of the plans I have, luv. G'night, guys. Don't wake us unless it's an emergency." He swatted Alexa on the ass.

Tay stood too, the need to check on Jaqui strong. "I'm turning in. Let me know if you hear anything."

Oz gave him the finger, while Dallas waved dismissively.

Outside the room he'd left Jaqui in, he listened for the sound of the shower running, but the doors were thick. He gave a knock. Waiting a full thirty seconds, he turned the knob before entering, then came to a stop in the entryway. There on the side of the bed lay Jaqui. Her hair was still wet from her shower, and she was sound asleep.

Gathering a pillow and extra blanket from the closet, he made himself a pallet between the bed and the door. He locked the door, then went into the bathroom for the quickest shower, looking down at his hard cock and ignored it. No way was he going to jackoff with Jaqui in the other room and too injured to do anything about it. He was a man of discipline, and his dick was going to learn to go without. Damn, it was going to be a long few weeks.

\*\*\*\*

Jaqui came awake at the sound of the shower coming on. Slightly disoriented, she held her breath, noticing the light from the bathroom, then remembered where she was. Her mind raced back to the last time she'd seen Taylor Rouland naked, and wished like all get out she could join him in the steamy shower. The aches in her ribs reminded her why she could do no such thing, and she got up to get a pain pill out of her bag. Looking around the room she realized she didn't have anything to swallow it down. The sound of the water shutting off was a relief, but also sent a little trepidation through her.

She looked down at herself. Wearing one of his T-shirts, she wondered if he'd be mad, or if he'd even notice. Feeling foolish as she stood by the bed, she sat down and waited.

Tay walked out, a towel wrapped around his hips. "What's wrong?" he asked, stopping to look around the dark room, light illuminating her.

"I needed to take a pain pill, but didn't have anything to drink. I didn't want to go to the kitchen so I thought I'd just wait for you to finish showering." She held her hand up, showing him the small pill in her hand.

He turned and went back into the bathroom, returning with a small paper cup filled with water. "Here you go. Do you need to eat anything before you take that?"

She showed him the little package of crackers. "I'm going to eat a couple of these first." The next couple minutes she spent eating, then popped the pill into her mouth, swallowing it and the water. "I hate taking pain meds."

The bed dipped as he sat next to her. "Me too, but you need the relief. If nothing else so you can sleep. Besides, you're safe here."

"I know." And she did. Tay and the other guys would risk life and limb for her. The heat from his body was like a balm to her soul.

"Why don't you climb under the covers and try to sleep. I'll be right down here if you need anything. Want me to leave the bathroom light on?" Tay eased up off the bed.

"Will you sleep with me? I mean hold me?" She was glad it was dark and he couldn't see the blush that stole up her face.

"Are you sure? I don't want to hurt you." His voice was a rough rasp.

The sound of his need matched her own. "Yes. I just need to feel you next to me."

"Damn, you undo me. Let me get dressed." He crouched down, coming up with some clothing and then disappeared into the bathroom

Jaqui wanted to tell him to not get dressed, but her poor abused body was not in any shape to handle anything other than holding. Gentle holding at that.

Tay came back out wearing a pair of basketball shorts and nothing else. Damn, the man was all six pack abs and gorgeous tanned skin. She'd seen him naked and had thought at the time he must've sunbathed nude, having seen no tan lines. The idea made her grin.

He walked around the bed, getting in on the other side and lying on his back. "I've never been as scared as I was when I heard you'd been taken." His deep baritone broke into her musings.

She didn't want to think about that time. "I thought you were on leave still?" That was why she had been in Columbia in the first place. They'd needed someone to break into the cartels security system, and they needed it done onsite since a remote location wouldn't work. Jose changed his password daily, but they'd found he was to be in town for the Carnival, and she knew if she was in close enough range, she could hack it. Just as Tay could have.

However, the doctors hadn't released him from his injuries. They'd assumed she'd be safe. She wasn't even in the same town as the kingpin or the SEAL team, hadn't even made inquiries. There should have been no way for the man to have known she was there, let alone what she looked like.

Leaning up on his elbow, he stared down at her. "If I'd known you were sent in my place, I'd have crawled over broken glass to get to you. When I found out you were...I couldn't get there fast enough. My heart felt like a vice was squeezing it. Until the moment I felt your own reassuring beat, until I knew you were going to survive, I didn't want to. You are the rainbow in my world. My ray of sunshine in an otherwise gray existence. Don't ever leave me again." His hand came up, almost hesitantly, then brushed damp strands from her forehead.

"You left me remember?" she pointed out in a whisper.

"Cause I'm a dumbass. I need you to make me a better man. Clearly you are not doing a good job." He smiled, the teasing clear in his rumble.

She wanted to reach up and touch his beard roughened face, but the little pill was starting to work. "I'll do my best to remind you of that daily. So tired, Tay."

"Sleep, my sunshine. I'll keep you safe."

"Hold me." Jaqui didn't care if she was pleading. After a near death experience, a girl had the right she assured herself.

"I'll be right next to you, but I don't want to hurt you."

She sighed, hearing his voice next to her relaxed all her muscles, mixed with the pain meds and she let herself go. "Mmkay," she mumbled.

\*\*\*\*

Tay kept the chuckle to himself. When he felt the tension leave Jaqui, he made sure she was covered, then allowed his own body to relax. Sleeping next to her was a form of heaven and torture mixed.

He woke to the feel of a warm weight pressed to his side. Yep, the next few weeks was gonna be his own form of hell.

Four weeks later...

Tay and Jaqui had moved to his cottage a mile down from Kai and Alexa. With the base having such a high security and no word from Medellin, they felt relatively safe doing so.

Every morning he got up, went on a jog to Polihale State Park and back. The nearly five miles pushed him, but made him feel like he was getting back to where he was before he was injured.

The alarm pad glowed red. Once he entered the code, he entered through the backdoor, intent on showering before checking in on Jaqui. Her bruising had faded to almost non-existent, and he hadn't seen her wince in over a week. It was becoming harder to lay next to her each night. Holding her was one of the things he looked forward to, yet he was also beginning to go to bed later, and get up earlier.

"Hey stranger." The woman of his dreams murmured, a coffee cup held up to her lips.

She looked delectable standing with her back resting against the counter wearing another one of his T-shirts. He realized she'd taken to using one of his concert shirts as her sleeping apparel, and damn if she didn't look sexier than a lingerie model wearing next to nothing. His mouth watered. "How are you feeling this morning?" He had to reach around her to grab his own mug, and was pretty sure she had placed herself in just such a position.

"Here, you can have the rest of mine. I just made it." She smiled up at him, a teasing light in her voice.

His dick got hard, or maybe it had been hard since the night he'd first slept beside her. Turning the cup around and placing his lips where hers had been, he took a sip. Closing his eyes at the refreshing taste of the rich brew, he hummed. "Delicious." He handed the cup back, but didn't step away. Only an inch or so separated their bodies. He could see the hard tips of her nipples pressing against the black material, making the band's name stick out a little more.

"You cold?" He asked, eyes dipping down then back up.

Her own eyes dipped below his waist, then back up. "Nope. You?"

"Sweaty, but far from cold, sunshine." He'd taken to calling her the term of endearment. The word fit Jaqui to a T.

She licked her lips. "I could use a shower, too. I feel a little sweaty coming on."

His brows pulled down. "Have you been overworking while I was out?" He sat the cup down, caging her in with his arms on each side.

"Excuse me, boss, but I do believe I can do what I want." She slapped a palm to his chest.

He looked at the delicate hand, happy there was no visible sign of the IVs anymore. The feel of her touching his bare chest made his heart rate increase. "Of course you can. I just don't want you out running or exercising without me is all," he consoled.

Her finger began tracing between his pecs, making him shiver. "No fair," he groaned.

"What's not fair?" she teased.

149

Holding onto his composure by a thread, he let her finger walk up his chest and encircle one of his nipples. "You're playing with danger. I haven't released the valve on this pressure cooker in weeks. You keep it up and I'm not gonna be responsible for what I do next."

She looked up at him. "You mean like this?" Then the little vixen pinched one flat disc between her fingers.

He looked at one of his favorite T-shirts that definitely looked better on her than him, and asked in a low growl. "You like that shirt, sunshine?" At her nod, he ran his palms down her sides until he reached the bottom. "You sure about this?"

"I'm not the one hesitating." She bent and licked the spot she'd pinched. All thoughts fled except getting her naked.

With his hands skimming up her thighs, he lifted the black shirt, exposing the boy cut panties she preferred. After they'd moved to his place, they'd ran over to her home and packed up several bags of her stuff. Things she said she had to have. He enjoyed all manner of panties, but agreed when she had said thongs had their purposes, but loved to see her in the lace trimmed briefs and nothing else.

What breath he had left, escaped him in a gush of air as he stared down at the tiny pair of pink boyshort undies she wore. "Damn, you are the sexiest thing I've ever seen." His palms smoothed up her ribs, careful of her even after all this time.

"I'm not going to break, Tay." Her hands brought his to her breasts, adding more pressure than he would have.

"You almost died." He ground out between his teeth.

"Almost only counts in horseshoes, and hand grenades," she whispered, then gasped.

Tay's mind short circuited. His head bent, his full focus on claiming Jaqui's lips like he had wanted since the first day he'd seen her, and every day since. There was no going back, no talking himself out of it. No sweet, tentative kiss. No, this was a hot, hard, all-consuming kiss that demanded she give him everything. She lifted onto her toes, and she opened her mouth as soon as his lips touched hers, allowing his tongue to sweep inside. Plundering, devouring. Her hands went to his biceps while he held her where he wanted her, and continued to sip from her.

She tasted like the rich coffee they'd drank, decadent and sweet. His sunshine. So damn sweet he feared he'd never get enough of her. His dick throbbed to be inside her, he burned to bury himself in all her goodness and be with her in every way imaginable.

With his mouth covering hers, he turned them toward the table in the middle of the kitchen. The old fashioned thing was made of solid oak, and was sturdy enough for what he had planned. He palmed her ass, and lifted until her ass was on the edge. Her breathing was just as hard as his when he broke the kiss. He parted her legs wide, making room for himself. The hard length of his cock pressed against the front of her panties through the thin fabric of his basketball shorts. Even through the material, he could feel how wet and hot she was and it made him harder.

Her legs came up and around him, and he shamelessly ground his dick against her. "Fuck, I love how you look right now." His thrust his tongue back inside her mouth, his hands palming her breasts, tweaking the pebble hard nipples. Her small, soft hands found their way beneath the elastic of his shorts. He groaned and released her mouth to press kisses to her neck, raking his teeth as he went.

Using his teeth and fingers, he plucked and teased, all the while his cock throbbed to the point of pain. He promised to keep himself in check until she was satisfied, and clenched his jaw. Her breasts were sensitive he remembered, and the thought of sliding his cock between the two mounds had him twitching against her.

"You're killing me here." Her blonde hair had come partially down from the bun she'd pulled it into, her skin was pale and smooth like peaches and cream.

She reached out to push his shorts down, but he stopped her before she could. "Not yet," he said, and when she looked ready to protest, he licked at one of her rosy nipples. "I plan to fuck you long and hard.

But if you put your hands on me, it's going to be over faster than I can decode a program."

Her arm dropped to the side of the table, making those beautiful breasts bounce.

Still standing between her spread thighs, the only thing separating them was those neon pink panties and his shorts, he tilted his head to the side as he stared into her cornflower blue eyes, and decided to ramp up the dirty. "What do you think about me making you my breakfast, sunshine?"

"Oh, god," she whispered. "I want that so bad. The thought of you licking me makes my body throb in all the right places."

Son of a bitch. A blush stole up her body, and all the breath left his lungs at her words.

He leaned back, and pulled the only thing covering her down her legs, dropping them to the floor.

Not wasting a minute, he moved back in and captured a nipple between his lips and tugged. He flicked the hard nub with his tongue, then moved to the other doing the same, then opening his mouth, he sucked as much of her inside as he could while kneading the other.

With one arm braced on the table, he trailed his hand down the flat planes of her stomach, sweeping his thumb across her swollen clit. She jerked against him, her cry of ecstasy music to his ears.

He pressed a finger inside her tight wet heat, adding a second as she began grinding against his hand.

"Tay, oh god, I'm going to, oh god," she cried out wildly, shamelessly rocking against him, fucking his fingers.

"That's it, baby. Reach for it." He loved that she was secure in her need and seeking her release, and felt it when her body was on the verge of splintering apart.

He bit down on her nipple when he was sure she was at the edge, sending her that final bit. Her body jerked, she gasped and her pussy locked down on his fingers while she rode out her first orgasm.

Her soft cry went straight to his dick, but he wanted, needed to taste her.

Holding her stare, he lifted his fingers to his mouth and licked her essence off one digit at a time. "You taste delicious, but I want more."

A strangled sound came from Jaqui, but she nodded.

\*\*\*\*

Jaqui was his willing slave in that moment. His dark voice had her face heating, a thrill of epic proportions shooting straight to the heart of her. Already her body was greedy for more.

"You could make a saint a sinner, Taylor Rouland."

His lips kicked up in a devilish grin. Those full lips she knew would give her so much pleasure. "Consider me your own personal devil, Ms. Wallace. Now you just lie there and let's see if I can get you to scream my name this time."

He hooked his foot on a chair and sat. The position put him at the perfect height, and left her completely open and vulnerable. He placed his big palms on her knees and widened her legs. She hadn't realized she'd closed them. Thick blond lashes gazed up at her. "Every inch of you is beautiful." He trailed his hands up the insides of her legs like a slow tease, making her stomach muscles tremble. His hot gaze telling her in no uncertain terms he was done talking.

Leaning back on her elbows, she bit her lip. Breathing became harder the longer he sat there staring, and then he lowered his head, placing an open-mouthed kiss at the top of her mound, his dark blue eyes locked with hers.

He lifted her legs over his shoulders, slid his hands around her hips, then down to her waiting pussy, the folds still soaking wet from her earlier orgasm. When he dipped his head, he spread the lips of her sex open at the same time, exposing her clit and rubbed the stubble of his chin against the sensitive bud, making her jerk. "Holy, shit." It was not enough, yet she knew he was going to give her so much more.

"Still not screaming my name." He blew a breath of air over the glistening folds. Her sex pulsed with renewed need.

As soon as the words left his mouth, he bent and she was hard pressed to stay upright. His mouth devoured her, licking and sucking with such masterful skill she didn't want to think where he'd learned the skills, couldn't think of anything except for the way he made her feel. Firm laps of his tongue along with the slight scrape of his beard, brought her close, but not quite there. "Please," she begged. She was nearly there, but needed more.

Slow, agonizingly slow, lazy lick after lick, and then his heated gaze met hers. "What's that?" he growled against her.

Oh, he was such a tease. She grabbed the back of his head. "Please make me come, Tay. I need to…"

She didn't finish her sentence before he'd latched onto her clit, massaging the pleasure point with the exact amount of pressure she needed. Two fingers slid through her, in her with ease, giving her that last bit of friction she needed, and her head fell back onto the hard table. Her hips lifted, riding his face and hands as ecstasy swept over her. "Yes, Tay, oh god, more," she swore.

Vaguely she was aware of him standing, and heard the chair scraping backwards as he stood and positioned the head of his cock against her. "You sure?"

"More than anything in the world," she whispered, the truth that was more than just words. Her world was a lot larger than what she'd allowed it. Sure, she'd jumped out of planes, and had been all over the world and back. But, she'd kept to her safe little bubble. Until Columbia. Now, she wanted to reach out and experience everything. If that included heartache again, then she'd survive, because she was a survivor, however she wasn't a quitter.

His air came out in a stream of breath like he'd been holding it in. Silly man. Here she was laid out, naked on his kitchen table, and he didn't realize she was a sure thing. He acted as if her answer meant as much to him as it did her. God, she hoped so.

Before she allowed herself to overthink things, she held her hand out to him. Wrapped her legs around his hips, wondering when he'd dropped the shorts, immediately forgetting everything except the feeling of him stretching her.

Damn, he only pressed a few inches inside, yet she felt deliciously full, needing more. She hadn't realized she said the word until he swore, then pulled back and pressed further inside.

"Jesus, sunshine, don't. I'm holding on by a thread. You keep talking like that and this is gonna be a hard, fast ride, not what I want for our first time in over a year." He swiveled his hips.

She lifted against him, squeezing her inner muscles. "You can make it up to me…next time. This time I want it hard and fast."

Her words were like waving a red flag at a bull. His nostrils flared, and then in the next instant he pulled almost all the way out, then shoved all the way in, eliciting a yell from her. It felt so damn good, it hurt, in a good way. Her body worked to accommodate him, memories of how sore she'd been for days after their time together flashed in her memory. Another cry tore from her throat as he pulled back, and powered back in, not giving her a chance to adjust to his size. Tay didn't allow her to catch her breath, just powered in and out, giving her exactly what she'd asked for, and she loved it.

With each downward thrust he hit her clit, pumping into her over and over, hard and deep, with a need that matched her own, increasing with each in and out thrust. His fingers bit into her hips, pushing and pulling her into him, making her meet each one of his strokes.

Lust overtook her as she arched her back, feeling her impeding orgasm swell inside her again. Shamelessly, she reached between their bodies.

"Fuck yeah, touch yourself. Let me feel you come on my cock." His guttural words sent a thrill through her. Then he lifted her by the hips, the new angle had him hitting a sensitive area inside her, and spots flashed before her eyes. It was too good.

Too much. So damn incredible she felt the need coil tighter between her thighs and deep within, her orgasm gathering force. "Right there, Tay. Yes, yes, yes," she screamed, her fingers flew over her clit.

"Damn, you're like a vice squeezing me. Fuck," he groaned, his voice a dark and intense rumble. He pushed her fingers out of the way and took over, pinching and tugging the needy flesh until it was too much and she pushed his hand away.

She felt him chasing his own pleasure as her own still pulsed through her, his hips ramming into her, his eyes such a stunning blue and raw with desire. The hard thrust rammed her into the table and she knew she'd have bruises, but they'd be the best kind. When his hips jerked, and he growled out his release, she held her arms out, feeling completely owned when he collapsed on top of her. Their hearts beat a furious staccato against their ribs.

"That was amazing, and by far the best breakfast I've ever had." He stood, their bodies still joined.

She liked having him on top where no part of her was left untouched by him. "I think we need a shower." His sweat glistened chest gleamed in the sunlight coming through the kitchen window.

"Thank goodness there's room enough for two." He pulled her into a sitting position, then eased out of her. They both looked down at the same time, noticing he'd not used a condom.

Her heart jerked, but returned to normal. "I'm on the shot, and I haven't had any partners other than you."

He shook his head as if clearing it. "I'm clean. I've never had unprotected sex and just had a checkup six months ago and you were the last woman I'd slept with."

The profound statement made tears form. She knew she'd waited her whole life for him, but hearing he'd not been with anyone else since her, was another link to the man who owned her body, soul, and mind. She feared if he left her, even though she said she was a survivor, she would crumble into a heap and not be the same again.

## Chapter Seven

Tay was dressed for work when Jaqui came out of the bedroom. She hadn't been cleared, and they'd been doing shifts of watching over her. He was sure she'd sleep in this morning after their day yesterday, followed by a drive up to Poipu Beach, where they'd swam and laid out in the sun for a few hours. When they'd returned home, he'd grilled them burgers while she made a salad and opened a can of baked beans. Each of them more interested in exploring each other, than what they put in their mouths. Well, his mind thought back to what he'd done to her on the kitchen table, and then what she'd done to him that night. God, his dick got hard thinking about her mouth and the delicious things she could do with it.

"Yo, Tay, mind out of the gutter man, I don't need to see that shit so early in the morning." Oz poured himself a cup of coffee.

He knew his hard-on was pressing against his fatigues, but images of a wet Jaqui on her knees with her lips wrapped around his cock was an erotic site to behold. The last thing he wanted to do was leave.

"I have to go home," Jaqui said, a stricken look on her face.

His hand stopped moving the cup up to his lips at her announcement. "What the hell are you talking about?"

She held her phone up, showing him her screen. Placing the mug on the counter he closed the distance between them. It took him a few moments to read through the text, then he looked into her watery eyes. Without thought, he pulled her into his arms. "It'll be okay." He felt Oz moving up to them, and handed him the phone.

"I missed the call, so my aunt texted me." Her voice wobbled.

Tay didn't want to say what he was thinking, but it was too coincidental that her parents were involved in an accident, yet it could happen. "I'll get cleared and we'll leave on the first flight."

Jaqui pulled away as much as he'd let her. "Tay, you don't have to come. I mean I want you to, but…" she stopped as he pressed his lips to hers.

"Ssh, I will be coming with you. Go shower and pack a bag. I'm going to head to base and get cleared." He made sure she heard he wouldn't take no for an answer.

Relief washed over her gorgeous face. "I'm going to call for an update." She pushed up on her tiptoes and kissed him.

He stared after her, the usual bounce gone.

"You've got it bad, man." Oz raised his cup, but no amusement laced his words.

Not seeing any reason to deny it, Tay nodded. "She's it for me. Don't know how or when it started, but I can't imagine waking up and not having her next to me."

"She likes to jump out of perfectly good airplanes too you know." Oz leaned against the table, his massive arms crossed, a twinkle in his eyes.

Tay raised his brows, but started for the door. "I'm aware of you corrupting her. I'll just have to make sure I'm with her next time." He turned before walking out. "Keep a close eye out today. My neck itches."

Oz nodded. "Mine too."

Commander Lee's office was a bustling hive of activity as Tay entered. He stood with his hands behind his back, waiting to be seen. Wasn't sure what he'd do if he didn't get cleared to go with Jaqui. The thought of giving up being a SEAL was one he hadn't entertained before, even when he'd been laid up in the hospital beaten to a pulp.

"The Commander is ready for you." The secretary announced.

"Thank you, ma'am." He entered his commander's office, seeing the older man staring at a map on the wall, posture straight as a pin.

"How's Wallace doing?" He asked without turning.

"Fine, sir. That's what I came here for. She's had a family emergency come up and is requesting leave. I'd like to go with her." There was no sense in pussy footing around when he knew Commander Lee would appreciate the lack of wasted time.

"I'm aware and agree. The incident stinks of sabotage. I hate to say this, but from the information I've gathered, the reason she was taken in the first place was because we have a leak. Her location, along with what she looks like was given to the cartel before she'd even arrived in Columbia. I hate to think this is more than just about Medellin, and more about Phantom Team. Or maybe the two are completely separate, but someone is manipulating things to get to their end game. Not many have access to the elite teams, but if they had Jaqui's info it could be because she's not part of your team." His Commander stared at something on his desk. "You go with her, and I'll have the rest of the team ready to go at a moment's notice." Commander Lee turned around, anger burning in his gaze and features.

Tay wasn't sure what he'd expected, but to see the usual stoic man showing so much emotion, wasn't it. He opened his mouth to respond, but was stalled by the commander raising his hand.

"Don't thank me just yet. I think we've stirred up a hornet's nest, and when you do that, you're liable to get stung as we've seen with what happened in Columbia to Jaqui. I don't want to see her get hurt again. Nor civilians like her family. I'm hoping I'm wrong, but I'm not usually. Damn it." He pounded his fist on his desk making several things bounce. "I should have anticipated this move from the cartel. They have her name and information. I just assumed they'd follow her here."

Shrewd dark eyes met his and he realized the commander had hoped the Bloque Cartel would have come after Jaqui. Anger boiled in his veins that the leader of his branch of the Navy, hadn't thought to include him on that little tidbit of knowledge. He wondered if Kai had been let in on it. The Bloque, or Block in English, Cartel weren't known for their forgiving ways. To have a captive, a woman at that, escape right from under them, would be seen as a weakness. One they wouldn't want the world to see, or they'd have others trying to move in on their territories.

"You knew they were looking for her and didn't share that with our team?" Tay tried to keep the accusation out of his voice, failing if the narrowing of Lee's eyes were to go by.

"Don't take that tone with me, boy. I'm in charge of this operation and do what I think is best. Now, unless you don't want to go with Wallace to visit her family…" his voice trailed off, clearly warning Tay he was on shaky ground.

His jaw ached from gritting his teeth, but he snapped his legs together and saluted the commander. "Sir, yes sir. We'll be leaving just as soon as we can get a flight."

"There's a flight leaving in one hour." Commander sat down in the chair, already dismissing him.

Tay nodded. "We'll be on it. Thank you, sir."

Commander Lee looked up, his lips tilted up in a slight grin. "That hurt a little, didn't it?"

"Only a little," he agreed.

"Go on then. You're down to fifty-eight minutes." Lee waved his hand and Tay saluted his commander before walking out.

He grabbed his cell and dialed Kai. As the phone rang, he thought of what he'd say if the leader of his SEAL team had known about the threat to Jaqui, and had kept him in the dark.

"Hey, Tay, what's up?"

The sound of metal clanging let Tay know where Kai was. If he'd had more time, he'd go to the workout center on base and talk with him face-to-face. "Did you know about the cartel and Jaqui?" He kept his voice down as he passed several people in the hallway.

"What do you mean did I know about the cartel and Jaqui? I was there when we rescued her, jackhole." A loud clang sounded at the end.

Tay filled him in on what he'd just found out from Commander Lee. Silence stretched with only the sound of a throbbing beat in his ear from whatever was playing in the gym.

"That's fucking bullshit. How the hell are we supposed to protect one of our own if we aren't informed? How am I supposed to lead a team if they don't trust I have their back?" Each word was growled, his deep voice menacing.

Tension left his body. "I'm going home with her, but he said he'd have you and the other guys ready to ship out if needed."

"Fuck that. We should go with you."

An image of Kai pacing flashed in his mind. "You stay here and keep your ears to the ground and spend some time with Alexa. We may need you sooner, rather than later." That was something he was sure was the truth, although he hoped like hell it wasn't.

\*\*\*\*

Jaqui stared at the clothes laying on the bed, unsure what to pack. Her mind and body felt numb.

Coming home from a late dinner, her parents' vehicle was hit in the middle of an intersection by a large pickup truck. Luckily for them a surgeon had been coming up behind and seen the accident and stopped to help. The other vehicle had fled the scene as he'd pulled up, leaving nothing but destruction to show he'd been there. Although she didn't think their small town had cameras on the stop lights, her mind raced to whether the local businesses might have security cameras. With the accident occurring right in the middle of Main Street she hoped at least one of them had a camera she could hack into and get a glimpse of the vehicle, and maybe the driver.

"What are you plotting?" Tay asked leaning against the door frame.

She had no clue how long he'd been standing there, but could kick herself for not paying attention to her surroundings. Actions like that could get her dead real quick. "I was thinking about how I could track down the hit-and-run vehicle."

Tay straightened, coming to stand next to her. "We will track him. Together. Feel me?" He pulled her against him. "Where you go I go. Until this is over, you are not to go anywhere alone, Jaqui."

A lump the size of a melon lodged in her throat. "You think someone tried to kill my parents, don't you?"

"I think it's a real possibility. They could have just been at the wrong place at the wrong time, or it could be Medellin and his men. Either way, you don't need to be alone. You are my heart, Jaqui. When I saw that jaguar lying on you, even before I knew it was you, I made a promise that I plan to keep, and that was I wouldn't fuck up again. If I have to super glue your ass to my side, I will do it."

She smiled in spite of herself. "You'd look a little silly with me in your dress uniform."

He gave her a little shake. "Don't. Please, for all that I hold dear. Don't. Fuck, woman. Don't you understand how much you mean to me? Feel that." He put her palm to his chest. "My heart belongs to you. If something happens to you, my heart may continue to beat, but I won't continue to live. Sure, I may still breathe, eat, and sleep, but I'll only be half a man because the other half of me is you. A man can't really be whole without the love of his life, and that is you for me."

"Taylor, you shit. I love you so damn much. You about killed me when you left and didn't come back. For the past year and a half I swear I tried to hate you. God, I tried. Now, with those words, you hold the power to destroy me. If anything happens to you I won't want to live. If you change your mind, I swear, I will hunt you down and..." she couldn't continue as he pulled her into his arms and covered her lips with his. The usual all-consuming kiss that ended in their lovemaking was missing, replaced with a poignant one that meant even more. Love poured from him to her.

"If we had more time I'd show you how much I love you. But, we have," he lifted his arm, looking at his watch. "Less than thirty-five minutes to pack and catch a flight. Commander Lee has us on the first one out."

She hugged him one last time. "He cleared you to go with me?"

"Yeah." He looked at the clothes lying on the bed. "You having issues deciding what to take?"

Knowing it was silly, she took a deep breath. "I'm nervous and being stupid. Both of which I'm not normally." Snapping out of the stupor she'd been in since getting the text, she started rolling outfits into neat little rolls, filling the case on the bed.

"I'll be ready in ten."

True to his word, Tay had a suitcase packed and ready in less time than she, and was waiting for her in the kitchen.

They locked up the house, and with both their cases and laptops, were on their way to the airstrip at Barking Sands Missile Range. They'd be flying into Nellis Air Force Base, just twenty minutes away from Vegas. The closer they got, the more she felt on edge.

"If you don't stop fidgeting you're going to make the other passengers nervous." Tay wrapped his fingers around her where they'd been twisting in the yellow fabric of the sundress she'd thrown on.

"I wish I could get an update on the flight." She bit her lip.

He reached around the back of her neck, the warmth of his palm on her bare skin sent a tingle of awareness through her. "We could join the mile high club," he suggested wickedly.

A laugh bubbled up. "Sure, could you imagine that getting reported back to our superiors?"

Tay sat in the center seat, with her near the window. He twisted a little blocking her from the view of those in the aisle. "You're right. That would probably raise some eyebrows. But this," he held her neck in one hand, while he trailed the other up her thigh under the hem of her dress. Leaning closer, he whispered in her ear. "You'll need to be quiet, sunshine."

She pressed her knees together, but the man's fingers slipping between the V of her thighs, had her wanting more. The blunt feel of his fingernail scraping over her clit had her arching forward, spreading her thighs wider, and giving him better access.

"That's it. Now, let's see how good I can make you feel," he growled too low for anyone else to hear.

He dragged his thumb back and forth, creating a hunger in her. When he reached for the edge of the lace and touched her bare folds, her hips jerked against his fingers and her breath hitched in her throat. Not compelled to stop there, he trailed his fingers through her wetness, then pushed two thick digits deep inside her and used his thumb to tease her clit in slow circles.

"Tay…" Her voice came out in a breathless whisper, conscious of others overhearing. Hunger pulsing through her veins and racing straight to the heart of her.

He bent and captured her next cry into his mouth, his fingers moving in and out of her faster, taking her up to a release that was both fast and hard.

He licked at her bottom lip, and muttered. "Let go, sunshine. I got you." The words and his actions had her falling into a kaleidoscope of colors.

Her breath came out in a shuddering gasp, and she wrapped one hand around his bicep, the other she pushed harder against the hand working in and out of her, holding him firmly in place as she came.

"Damn, I can feel your tight little pussy squeezing my fingers with every pulse of your heart. I can't wait to have my cock in here so you can clasp every inch of me. I'm going to fuck you so deep, and hard, you and I will be lost to everything and everyone for that moment in time."

\*\*\*\*

Tay shook with the need to replace his fingers with his dick. Jesus, he could stare into her cornflower blue eyes forever, but especially when she came. The savage need he had for this woman took pleasure to a whole new level, making it so damn fierce, he literally shook with the restraint it took to pull his fingers out of her pussy, and not jerk her on top of him.

He took his fingers that were coated in her juices, and let her watch as he sucked them clean. Heat flared in her face, a rosy hue covered her skin. One he knew would cover her from head to toe.

"You are a dirty man, Taylor Rouland," she said huskily.

A laugh broke free from him. "You say that like it's new news to you, sunshine."

She ran her hand over his jaw. "I wish I could repay you. Thank you seems lame."

He adjusted the visible bulge in his jeans. "You can take your turn later."

"That's a promise. For now, I need to go to the ladies' room." She looked up at the front of the plane. "How much longer do you think we have before we land?"

Looking at his watch he was surprised to see they were close. "If you need to go, you better do it now. I'd say within the next half hour we should start our descent."

Tender emotion for his woman hit him again as they stood, and he watched her walk toward the front. He looked around him, checking out the other passengers and noticed several watched the sexy sway of Jaqui's hips as she passed. None were close enough to have seen or overheard him pleasuring her, but if they looked close enough they'd see a satisfied woman. And she was his. He didn't care that he was being possessive. He sat back down and waited, keeping his eye trained to the front. He'd lived a shallow life before her. Not that his life as a SEAL was anything other than fulfilling. Pride for what he did filled him. Sensing her approach, he looked up and smiled, his heart literally squeezed in his chest at the answering smile. She was so damned sexy, her yellow flirty dress fit her like a glove across the chest all the way down to her hips, flaring out to just above her knees. The wedge shoes she put on gave her an extra couple inches, and added to her sleek frame. He'd prefer her out of the clothes, but given their current circumstances, he'd appreciate the way she looked, knowing he'd have her later.

"Feel better?" He stood for her to slide in, setting aside his dirty thoughts for the time.

She settled onto the seat beside him, picking up her bag from under the seat in front of them. He watched as she applied lotion on her hands. "I swear the soap in the bathrooms are designed to rub the skin off your hands."

Tay had to agree, shaking his head when she offered him some of her sweet smelling lotion. She rolled her eyes, which made him smile. He enjoyed their light easy banter, something he'd only ever had with his SEAL team members. The flight attendant announced they were beginning their descent, so he and Jaqui sat in comfortable silence. When they landed, he stood and grabbed both their bags from the overhead compartment, then waited for Jaqui to grab her bag, shrugging his backpack with his laptop in it on his back, he offered to take hers as well.

"I've got this." She tapped her messenger bag shaped like a large leather book.

Slipping a hand around her neck, he tipped her head back toward his. "Of course you do," he murmured, loving the shock on her face as he sealed his lips over hers, kissing her. Slowly, thoroughly. Leaving no part of her lips and mouth unclaimed.

She shivered, her hip rubbing against his dick, her tongue tangled seductively with his until they were both breathless and aroused. He could easily picture stripping the clothes off her and having his way with her on the nearest flat surface here and now. But they'd come to Vegas for a purpose. And he needed to get his body under control or he'd be giving all the people in the terminal an eyeful.

"They're moving." He indicated with a nod of his head toward the aisle.

She straightened her shoulders, determination in every line. "I want to go directly to the hospital."

He had figured as much. Would have wanted to do the same thing. "We'll rent a car and make that our first stop. You want to call your aunt now, or wait until we get to the rental place?"

She bit down on her lip again. "I'll wait until I can tell her a more accurate time. Besides, I don't want to be rushed when I speak to her."

They were walking as she spoke, his eyes looking left and right. Simmering just below the surface was a rage he'd kept controlled since he'd realized Medellin had taken Jaqui. Now, he channeled that anger, turned it into a weapon he could use. Their two carry-on bags were stacked together as he wheeled them, leaving his right hand free. He didn't have a weapon, yet. However, he planned to rectify that with a phone call, knowing his Commander would have cleared him since this was an official case. Sort of.

They were quickly given an SUV at the car rental counter. Being in the Navy had its perks, and luckily the guy was the son of a retired army vet. He waited for Jaqui to call and get an update, having sent off a text to Kai, and was told there was going to be a duffel waiting for him at the hospital.

She hung up, her chin dropping to her chest. He didn't like the quiet, serious mode, but knew she had a lot on her mind.

"They're both stable, still in the ICU, but are expected to be moved to regular rooms. I want them in the same room, damn it." She took a shuttering breath.

Knowing she was only thinking with her heart, not her head he kept quiet. Tay couldn't believe that it had been only a couple months ago, he was living with the notion he didn't need a woman in his life. He glanced over at the silky blonde hair pulled back in a long ponytail of the woman he loved, trying to imagine his life without her. "Let's just take it one step at a time. When we get there, we'll talk to the people in charge and see if we can't arrange it." He put his hand over hers. She immediately gave him her undivided attention. "Hey, if we keep our cool and speak to them with logic, they'll listen. If not, I'll become the big bad SEAL."

A soft giggle escaped. "I love it when you get all badass. It's pretty sexy," she breathed out.

"Bottom line, we will do it together, sunshine. Don't think to go off halfcocked, and remember what I said about staying next to me." His stomach knotted as images of what she'd gone through the last time she'd been at Medellin's mercy.

She nodded her agreement, her eyes taking in the scenery in that introspective way of hers he loved.

Tay had no doubt her sharp mind was already working through scenarios, trying to figure out ways around the red tape they may encounter. He hoped like hell he wouldn't have to do any hacking into the hospitals system to get what they wanted. A legitimate move would be best, but he'd do it if it meant making the Wallace family happy. Happy wife, happy life was a phrase he'd heard often and agreed with wholeheartedly.

They parked at the Summerlin Hospital Medical Center with its gorgeous backdrop of the mountains behind it. He hopped out, rounded the bumper to open Jaqui's door. She raised her brow, but gave him her hand. The hospital was located in one of the wealthier areas, and he wondered if her parents were well off. Other than knowing Jaqui the Navy officer, and the woman, he didn't know too much about her family. Their names, and that she was originally from Las Vegas about summed up his knowledge of her family.

"What does your dad do for a living?" He asked, the doors to the main entrance opened in front of them before she could answer.

"He owns a construction business and my mom is a hair dresser. Or she was. Now, she is semi-retired." Each of them had their laptop bags, but had left their suitcases locked in the rental car.

"How is one semi-retired from hair dressing?" He quizzed.

She glanced his way. "She owns a shop, but doesn't work there and only does certain clients hair. Um, you'd understand if you saw her at her best."

Understanding hit him. Her mother would normally be all dolled up. "Hey, I'll see her fixed up sooner than you think."

A watery smile met his words. They went to the information desk to get directions. In a hospital the size of Summerlin they'd need them. "Yes you will."

# Chapter Eight

She was a ball of nerves walking into the ICU. The gnawing worry over her mom and dad was new and unwelcome. Her dad was always larger than life in her eyes, while her mother was more like her.

Once they reached the Intensive Care Unit, she was holding Tay's hand like the lifeline it was. Their first roadblock came in the form of the woman manning the front desk. After Jaqui explained who she was there to see, she was told only two visitors were allowed in at a time. Her mind couldn't figure out who could be there other than her aunt and uncle on her mom's side.

"How about my dad? May I see him then?" She blinked back the burn of angry tears.

The lady took more time than Jaqui felt was necessary, looking through whatever she had on her screen, before she cleared them through. Although the rules said only two visitors per patient, the first room she came to was her mother's. The sight of her aunt and uncle made her stop in her tracks. Her brief glimpse in let her know her mom was awake.

No amount of rules would stop her from seeing her mother. "Mama," she cried out rushing into the room.

Her relatives stood, but didn't try to stop her when she rushed to the side of the bed. "Baby girl," Maci winced.

"I'm so glad you're awake," Jaqui said in a hushed whisper.

Her mother's right arm, along with her right leg was in a cast from the impact of the vehicle being struck on the driver's side, and then pushed into the light pole. More tubes ran from her mother than she had from her own injuries only weeks ago. They'd had to re-inflate her lung as well, and only through the saving grace had a doctor been on that road, otherwise her parents may have died.

"They just took the tube out of her throat so she's a little sore," her Aunt Laci murmured.

Jaqui adjusted her bag behind her. "You don't need to talk, mom. I'm just glad you're going to be okay. You and dad both are." She smiled down at the scraped face of the older version of herself, afraid to touch any part of her mother.

"Do you want some more water?" At her mom's nod Laci continued. "We can dip these swabs in water and let her suck on them, but they don't want her to have too much yet."

Her aunt looked over at Tay, then back at her. "Mama, I'm gonna check on daddy, then I'll come back. They have this silly rule about only allowing two of us in at a time. I'm already breaking rules and I've been home for less than two hours."

Her mother smiled then grimaced. "When is she due for her next pain dose?"

While her aunt pressed the nurse call button, Jaqui and Tay went to check on her dad. Lance Wallace wasn't as big as Tay, but to her he was a man above men. He had brown hair with natural blond highlights and gray eyes. Years of working construction had given him a muscular physique that most men twenty years his junior envied. Walking into his room was a lot different than the one with her mom. Her dad didn't have as many tubes hooked to him, nor any visible casts. However his issue was the fact he'd been knocked unconscious and they had to drill a hole in his skull to release fluid that had built up.

"He looks so...still. My dad is never one to lay about." That wasn't the only thing wrong. His normal tanned skin had a pale, almost gray tinge to it.

Tay gave her a reassuring hug. "Hey, he's a fighter right? I mean he has to be to have a daughter like you."

"Damn right I am." The scratchy voice, that sounded like he'd smoked one too many cigarettes, of her dad, had her stepping away from Tay.

"You scared the crap out of me." She pressed a gentle kiss to his forehead.

Her dad reached up and held her head to his. "I always said you had too much crap in you, sprite."

She'd always been his sprite. The familiar teasing made the tears she'd held at bay roll, wetting her dad's face in the process. She tried to stand, but he held her with the strength she relied on. "Love you, Daddy."

"Love you to the moon and back, my sprite. Now, who do you got with you?" Knowledge flicked in his eyes.

"Hello, Mr. Wallace. My name is Taylor Rouland, sir." He came to stand next to Jaqui, holding a tissue in his hand.

She glanced at the tissue and then her dad, then laughed, using the tissue to dry the tears on his face first. She wasn't sure if they were all hers. Was pretty sure he'd cried a little, but he wouldn't admit it. "Tay, this is my dad. Dad, this is Tay."

"You can call me Lance as long as you're good to my baby girl. However, if you break her heart, then you'd better make sure you can run real fast," her dad said with heat.

"No problem, Lance. I can guarantee you I'll treat her like the precious thing she is."

"Good," he muttered.

"Hello, I'm right here."

They both glanced at her, then shrugged.

After a little while she could tell her dad needed rest more than company. "We are going to drop our bags off, then grab some dinner and come back. By then, hopefully both you and mom will be moved to regular rooms."

"You going to stay at the house?" He questioned, looking between them both.

"No, I want to be close to you and mom." She stopped as he held up his hand.

"Now, listen to me. You can go home and sleep in your own bed for the night and be here in the morning. There's no reason to stay at a hotel where thousands of people have stayed, and done god knows what on them beds." Her dad gave his best no nonsense glare.

"Fine, but just so you know, I have stayed at hotels before." She stuck her tongue out at him.

Lance put his hand on his heart. "My child has been corrupted. Go on. Give your mom a kiss for me before you go."

She leaned in and gave him a kiss on his whiskered cheek. "I will. Love you."

"Love you more."

Walking back out, she felt lighter. Her aunt was still in with her mom. "We are going to drop our bags off at the house, grab a bite to eat, and fingers crossed, they'll both be in a regular room when we get back. Dad wanted me to give mom a kiss, but since she's sleeping I'll give it to you." She drew her aunt in for a big hug. "Thank you for staying with mom and being here when I haven't been."

Laci waved her words away. "Oh, palease. You are off serving our country. Girl, we are all so damn proud of you, especially your mama. And that hunk you have with you." She nodded toward Tay standing in the hall. "If they made all Navy men look like that, I'd sign up right now."

Jaqui slapped her aunt. "You're bad, Aunt Laci. Besides, Uncle Dave wouldn't make it in the Navy, he's afraid of large bodies of water."

Laci snorted. "I know. How silly. Oh well. It's a good thing I love that man."

She loved her family. They were goofy, loving, and all things a good family should be. If Jose

Medellin had succeeded, she didn't know what she'd have done. "Make sure you don't go anywhere alone, and don't accept things from strangers." The need to warn against anything that might seem suspicious hit her.

"Jaqui, we better go," Tay announced.

"Sweetheart, I am aware of my surroundings. Don't you worry, I'll see you in a few hours." Her aunt winked outrageously.

Tay stood with the casual appearance of a man who knew two women were talking about him. He held a large, hard, black case that she knew held weapons of some sort. He gave a brief nod, then led the way back toward the SUV. The big SEAL was in place, his gaze taking everything and everyone in that they passed. Her own anxiety rose the closer they got to the vehicle, and she watched as Tay looked it over. When he opened the case and pulled a device out, she realized the threat to her parents and her life was real. Watching as he ran a wand over and around the vehicle, then unlocked her door.

She couldn't believe her life had come to checking her vehicle for bombs. The reassuring heat of Tay's hand over hers had her looking up. He looked tense, but in control.

"It's going to be fine. I'm just taking extra precautions where you are concerned," he rushed to reassure her as if knowing she needed it. He inhaled a deep breath then released it, which seemed to ease some the tension from his body. "I've got your parents' address programmed into the GPS. You ready to roll?"

Nodding, she twisted her hand around and gave his a squeeze. "Yeah, I am."

They remained quiet for the short drive from the hospital to the gated community where her family home was located. It dawned on her that an intruder would need to know the access code to get inside, or be very good at getting around the security guard, or kill him. The last made her shiver. "Should we warn the staff at the gate not to let anyone in, who doesn't have a legitimate reason that is backed by a resident?"

The eyes lit up making them bluer, his expression turned thoughtful. It was one she recognized from when he was planning a mission, but now he was directing toward her protection. Everything inside of her that was a woman reacted to that heated gaze. Her heart that already belonged to him raced while her body ached to be possessed by him.

At the guard shack, he glanced down at her nipples, seeing how they were poking out against the yellow sundress and gave her a wolfish smile. When he met her gaze he gave her a wink. "I'm on it."

The double entendre didn't escape her. Heat suffused her, but she had to admit, the man definitely knew how to get her mind off the matter at hand. Passing her identification over to the young man at the gate, they waited while he ran her information through the system.

"Dang, this is a really upscale neighborhood," Tay said under his breath.

"My dad worked hard to build up his construction business and if you listen to him, he got lucky. However, me and my mom can attest to the fact he busts his ass, and doesn't mind getting his hands dirty to this day." She said a little more testily than she'd planned.

Tay leaned over the arm rest. "Sweetheart, I know you and your family are salt of the earth. I didn't mean anything by my comment."

Blowing out a breath, she gave him a sheepish smile. "Sorry, I think I'm a little on edge."

****

Tay was pretty sure he knew what was bothering Jaqui, but nothing short of capturing Medellin would completely ease her fears. Her calm, focus, and composed world, the same type of world he preferred was completely knocked off its axis, and she was struggling. He'd learned how to cope with upheavals in his life, whether it was on a mission, or personal. Now, he zeroed in on how he could help Jaqui relax.

While they waited he went through a mental check list of what he needed to do in securing her home. From the looks of the community, it could be a nightmare.

The home they pulled up to once the guard cleared them was a sprawling one story home on a large plot of land. If he had to guess he'd say they had close to an acre lot, one of the largest in the cul-de-sac.

"FYI, my parents have a state-of-the-art alarm system, so you can stop worrying so much. Oh, and pull up to the garages. I'll have to get out and punch in the code to open it." Jaqui smirked and gave him a long appraising look.

"How about you give me the code and I'll unlock the garage." He shrugged. "It's a control thing."

He didn't want to allow her out in the open. Not that his internal alarm was going off. His inner caveman was rearing its ugly head. Damn, he had it bad.

Understanding glimmered in the cornflower blue gaze she leveled at him. "Look, you know I am a

Navy officer too right? I mean, I can usually handle myself in most situations, not to mention, I can kick some ass."

Tay swallowed the instant denial before admitting the truth. "I'm afraid. Afraid to lose you again."

"You won't lose me. Remember, we are gonna be stuck together like glue. But, I need to be able to do things without you hovering like a helicopter boyfriend," she stated bluntly.

Tay swore beneath his breath. "How about a lawnmower boyfriend." At her raised brows, he replied. "You know, the one who mows shit down for you? I am so on board for that roll."

She laughed. "That's a new one. I do love you, Tay, and I appreciate you wanting to be there for me and do those things." She held up her hand. "But, you will not always be around. What happens when you have to leave for a mission? I'm an independent woman. I need to be able to stand on my own two feet like I've always done. Something terrible happened to me, but I survived. We can't allow Medellin or the

Bloque Cartel to take any more from me or the people I love." Her voice quivered on the last.

As scary as it sounded, Tay knew it was true and nodded in agreement. He didn't like it, but he understood what she was saying.

The home they entered was certainly expensive, but comfortable looking. He followed behind Jaqui, all too aware of their surroundings. The home was a security nightmare with the front having a fuckton of windows that he was sure weren't bulletproof, not to mention he counted several entry and exit points and he'd only come in through the garage.

"What has that frown on your face?" She asked, looking over her shoulder.

"There are a fuckton of security risks in this place." He had to forcibly swallow back the rest of his demand for them to leave and stay at a hotel.

She stopped in the middle of what appeared to be the entryway or foyer. "So, I'm assuming a fuckton is more than a shitton?"

He narrowed his eyes, sure she was laughing, yet she didn't crack a smile. "Abso-fucking-lutely. I mean, look at this place. Who cleans the damn windows for crying out loud?"

The little minx did laugh then. A full belly one that had her doubling over. Tay thought he'd wait her out and lay out all the reasons the home was a security risk. When she didn't seem in any hurry to stop, he tossed his hands in the air. "Are you done yet?" He asked.

Jaqui seemed to be trying to catch her breath, and that was when he became aware she must know something he didn't. "Alright, spill."

"I love it when you get all caveman on me. Like, seriously." She wiped under her eyes tears of mirth. "I was waiting for you to toss me over your shoulder and head back to the SUV." When he made a move toward her, she held her hands up in front of her, laughing. "Okay, I'm stopping. My dad didn't have bulletproof windows installed per say, but they are the next best thing, Tay. We have glass-clad polycarbonate bullet resistant glass on all the windows. He got a great deal on them when he built the factory for the maker of the glass."

Tay glanced around the dark interior of the home, appreciating the Wallace's money now more than ever. The place was spotless, and large, but not overly grand. "Do you have a housekeeper, and cook?"

Again, the woman of his dreams laughed. "Okay, I'm stopping," she said. "Yes, my mom has a cleaning lady who comes in once a week to do the deep cleaning, but she does the everyday stuff. As for a cook, forget about it. My mama loves to cook, and make no mistake, that is her domain."

He held the case with the weapons that were dropped off for him securely in one hand, and waited for Jaqui to lead the way to her room. "Let's go princess. I want to drop this off and then maybe we can whip up something to eat."

Her room was exactly what he'd pictured it would be. A large bed covered with a coral bedspread was against one wall with white wood furniture that looked like feminine masterpieces. Over the head of the bed sheer drapes hung as if framing the headboard, and he had an insane urge to use the ends to tie her up. She wheeled her suitcase in and placed it at the foot of the big bed. He followed, stopping a breath away. "I am imagining all kinds of things I'd like to do to you in this bed," he whispered, grinning down at her upturned face.

"Oh, are you now? Why, that is scandalous." She tapped her lips. "Do you know I've never brought a boy back here?"

"Newsflash, sunshine. I'm not a boy." He pulled her to him with one hand on the nape of her neck. He knew how much she enjoyed it when he exerted that slight bit of authority.

She nodded. "Believe me, I know. God, do I know." Licking her lips, she tucked her hand into the front of his jeans, the slim fingers touching his bare skin had him groaning.

"If you want to eat, you better stop teasing." The soft touch of her fingers sliding back and forth on the bit of flesh beneath the waist band where she'd tucked them had him hard as steel. A fact she was clearly enjoying and unable to miss as those fingers touched the head of his cock.

"I am a little hungry," she said, then blew his mind as she unfastened his belt, followed by the top button.

"Easy there. I don't have a thing between me and my jeans."

Her eyes flared at his clear meaning.

She shook her head. "You went commando? You dirty boy."

Tay fisted his hand in the ponytail making her tip her head back. "I'll show you I'm a not boy. On your knees, sunshine."

Oh yeah, his little sunshine loved it when he got bossy. At the foot of her king sized bed, she swiftly dropped to her knees, the fluffy rug cushioning her knees. Slowly, she eased the zipper down. The relief he felt as she spread the sides of his jeans open, was cut short by her hand engulfing him in a tight fist.

He wrapped his hand around hers and showed her how hard and fast he liked it, pumping his erection up and down, once, twice, three times in a slow practice move, until a bead of precome appeared on the slit.

Her eyes locked on what they were doing, and then she licked her lips. Damn, he didn't think he'd last long once she put her mouth on him. He watched as she shifted and knew she was as turned on as him.

"Open your mouth and take me inside, sunshine." He rubbed the head against her bottom lip, and she licked away the small drop from the tip, then her bottom lip, making him groan loudly. "Fucking hell, I need to feel your hot mouth taking me in. Suck me baby, slide that soft tongue all the way down my cock." His words were harsh, the fist in her hair flexed.

"I've never done this before, but I've read lots of books, and watched a few movies." Before he could ask her any questions, she moved forward.

The hands she'd had at her sides came up and gripped his thighs and she opened wide, allowing him to push his dick inside. He wasn't about to go too far, but the firm grip she had on him pulled him in farther, making her take him all the way inside to the back of her throat, then she pushed him back, controlling his movements. The hard suck on the crown had his eyes crossing. She repeated the process again and again. The slow glide in, then the slower glide out, followed by the exquisite suck, made him curse long and hard. Bracing his hand in her hair, he guided her in the pace and rhythm he needed, taking over control, and she let him, of that he had no doubt.

In no time he was racing toward orgasm, felt it flowing from his toes clear to the roots of his hair. His thrusts grew harder, less controlled, and she took it. Took him, and amped it up by reaching between his legs, palming his balls. "Fuck, yes, god damn, Jaqui, love you...fuck," he shouted.

His body shook, and when she took him to the back of her throat and swallowed around him, he was lost. "Gonna come. Your mouth is the best. Fucking love it. I'm sorry...can't stop." He tried to breathe, felt his dick pulse and her tongue lick, and then his hips continued jerking erratically through his orgasm. Words flew from him, raw shouts of ecstasy and love. When he was sure he had nothing left to give, he released the fist in her hair, running a palm over the poor abused scalp.

She glanced up, arousal simmering up at him. Her tongue came out and licked those lips that had just given him so much pleasure, then she kissed his abdomen. He had no clue when his shirt had come off, or where he'd tossed it. A siren's smile graced her pleased face.

He locked his knees and bent, pulling her up so they were face to face with his hands around her ribs. Without hesitating he covered her mouth with his. After he had his fill, he leaned back. "That was amazing. Your mouth should be illegal."

A sweet smile curved her lips. "Well, it's a good thing you're the only one who knows."

The possessive way he felt had him eyeing the bed behind her. "You better believe it." He didn't see any reason to deny it. "Let's break that bed in. Shall we?"

She laughed. "You truly are a dirty SEAL, Tay. Do your superiors know that about you?"

# Chapter Nine

Off the charts anticipation licked at her when he gave her an arrogant grin. She swore there was so much in the curve of his lips, and her body literally vibrated from giving him pleasure.

"Wrap your legs around my waist, sunshine."

His order increased her excitement, but she hesitated. With his bare skin, and her wrapping around him, he was sure to feel how wet she was.

"Why are you hesitating?" He cocked his head to the side.

"I'm wet," she admitted.

He grinned. "Ah hell, I want to get your sweet cream all over me. Believe me, before I'm finished, I plan to have it dripping from my lips to my chin and anywhere else it happens to land."

"You make it sound like I'm going to gush." She buried her face in his neck.

Tay let her down his body until she stood on not quite steady legs. "Baby, I'm going to make you come so many times, you are going to be drenched."

Her breath escaped in a rush. "How the hell did I go without you for so long?"

Trailing a finger down her healed cheek, he bent and pressed his lips to her ear. "You were waiting for me to realize what an idiot I was. Thank god I finally pulled my head out of my ass, sunshine." His hand brushed the strap down on her dress, first on one side, then the other. The bodice caught on her nipples, making him growl. "Amazing. I plan to savor every inch of you." A slight nudge and her dress fell to her waist, leaving her in a strapless bra.

She wiggled, and raised her hands to push the fabric down, but he stopped her. "You're my present to unwrap." Reaching behind, he unfastened the bra, tossing it to the side. His hands trailed down her sides, easing the dress down and her panties with it. His hands lifted her out of the puddle of material, leaving her in the strappy shoes.

Then he shocked her by dropping to his knees, and unbuckling the straps. She had to press her knees together for fear she'd shove herself into his face. Goodness, she was ready for him and his talented body. Any part of his body. Fingers, tongue, or that glorious cock she'd just had in her mouth.

"You weren't lying when you said you were wet. Damn, you are so damn sweet," he said softly. "I love that I'm the only man who's seen this pussy."

Looking down, it amazed her they'd swapped positions, yet she felt exposed. His commanding look was back. "Spread your legs for me. Let me make you come."

She obeyed, moving her legs about a foot apart, but Tay wasn't about to let her get away with that. The demanding man used his palms on the insides of her knees and forced her to step wider.

Her fingers sank into the bedding behind her for balance as he sat back on his haunches and stared at her.

"Look at you. All open and swollen for me." He leaned forward, licking up her inner thigh. "Your

211

folds part like a flower, and the lips of your sex are glistening with your juices. Makes me feel ten feet tall knowing you get just as hot for me as I do you." His hands slowly glided up her inner thighs, making her whimper when he finally reached the apex of her legs. He brushed the tips of his thumbs along the crease, causing all her nerves to stand up.

"Oh god, Tay, don't tease me," she begged.

"What do you want me to do?" He turned gleaming eyes up at her, satisfaction in the blue depths. "Tell me. Do you want me to lick you, or suck your clit, or would you rather I use my fingers?" he asked as he traced a wet trail of open mouthed kisses across the top of her mound, yet stopped short of where she needed him. "I need you to tell me exactly what you want and how you want it."

"Yes. All of it. Lick me, suck me and fuck me with your fingers." She didn't care that she was begging.

"One more question, sunshine. Do you want it slow or fast? Hard or soft? I guess that's two," he chuckled against her.

"All four damn you." Her body was ready to explode.

His hot breath feathered over her wet folds. "Your wish is my command." He breathed before he parted her lips with his fingers and did just that. Sucking, licking and fucking her in slow and fast passes. His tongue curled around her clit, then swooped down and lapped at her opening, making her arch toward him in greedy pleas. Teasing swirls and furious thrusts with his tongue, the deliberate licks and strokes had her racing toward a release. When he pushed two thick digits into her, she shamelessly grabbed the back of his head, holding him to her. He latched onto her clit and sucked the bundle of nerves, using that diabolical tongue and his teeth to drive her over the edge. Her body jolted and she cried out his name while he continued to lick until he wrenched every drop from her.

She felt him stand, but her ass had fallen onto the edge of the bed. With her body still buzzing, she wasn't sure how much time had passed, but when she opened her eyes, Tay stood before her gloriously naked. His huge cock on display.

He was so damn comfortable in his nudity, and way too good looking. All hers. His cock jerked beneath her gaze, curving upward toward his lower abdomen. A renewed thrum of need pulsed through her.

"Climb into the middle of the bed. I don't think I will last if I get my hands on you again." He tipped his head.

Rolling over, she crawled into the middle of the bed, slowly, seductively, her body moving like a sinuous cat. She made sure to put some extra swing in her hips, and looked over her shoulder, reveling in the fact he was every bit as affected by her as she him. By the time she reached the middle of the bed, he'd climbed on and knelt behind her.

The heat of his body covered her from behind. "You like to play?" Having him crowded up behind her should have scared her. Instead, it had her heart thumping in anticipation.

"Only with you," she whispered breathlessly.

Tay ran his hand down her back, over her upturned ass and between her thighs. "Only with me is right."

Oh, God. She swallowed as he pushed into her, bracing her hands and knees apart, feeling a rush of cool air as he sat back. His hands held her hips, and she instinctively pushed back, wanting to take more even though that initial entry caused her to whimper.

"You okay?" He held still with his cock buried inside her.

Nodding, she exhaled. "Better than okay. Fuck me, Tay. I want to feel you long after you're no longer in me."

"Jesus Christ," he growled. "Don't say shit like that." His body vibrated with an echoing need in her.

"I know what I want, and I want it hard and fast. I'm not breakable remember." She rolled her hips, squeezing her internal muscles.

From one second to the next, he went from not moving to pistoning in and out, shoving so deep inside her, she couldn't stop the shocked cry from exiting her throat. In this position she felt full, fuller

215

than she'd ever been and her body tried to adjust to the invasion, and the sensations he was lighting up.

She dropped down to her elbows, her breath coming out in gasps, but Tay didn't let up. Pumping into her fast and furious, with a need that increased with each pulsing thrust. His big hands pulled her back to meet his pistoning hips again and again, the pounding strokes hitting her right where she needed deep inside.

It was raw and dominating, and she loved it. Loved him, and gave herself over to the feelings he drew from her with his body. Lust overtaking her, she cried out, shaking, pushing back against him. Behind her closed lids, stars flashed, making the ache between her thighs increase. So close. The need coiling tighter, just out of reach.

Tay, attuned to her body, reached between her thighs, and rubbed the bundle of nerves in time to his thrust. "Come for me. Now," he demanded his voice dark and along with the thrusts and the hand between her thighs, she couldn't deny him.

"Yes, Tay. Don't stop, please." She shoved back against him.

"Never." She knew he was promising more, but then her release slammed into her, and she screamed, the flood of pleasure rippled over her uncontrollably.

A deep possessive male groan followed her as he rammed into her a few more times, his fingers biting into her hips. Jaqui loved knowing she would be wearing his marks, and they'd be the only ones to know it.

Unable to hold herself up, she dropped down to her stomach, with Tay's hands still holding her partially.

"Let me take care of you." The slight pain as he pulled out felt delicious.

She shook her head and tried to move forward up the bed. "Can't move," she muttered.

His masculine chuckle was followed by the bed dipping slightly as he got up and got a wash cloth. Once he cleaned her up, he climbed back onto the bed "Let's just lay here for a while. You wiped me out, too"

Goosebumps rose on her flesh. Tay, always on alert, pulled the comforter they'd somehow shoved down over them, then snuggled up against her. "Love you, Tay. Thank you for coming with me."

"I told you I'd always come for you, sunshine. You know that song about sunshine. You truly make me happy. My days were gray before you. If you listen to that song, really listen to it, it says exactly how I feel. I begged all that was holy not to take my sunshine away. He's given me another chance, and I'll do anything to keep you safe."

She turned, tears falling from her eyes. "That is one of my favorite songs. My mom used to sing it to me as a kid. Now, it has a whole new meaning." She wrapped her arms around him. "Hold me and don't let me go."

"For as long as you will have me, I'll always be here. You're my one." He kissed away her tears. "Okay, enough of the crying. We're too tired to explore the only type of wet I will allow you to get."

"So bossy." She snuggled closer. His warmth, and soothing motion of his palm on her back lulled her into a restful sleep.

****

Tay woke. A strange sound penetrated his sleep. He pressed a finger to Jaqui's lips. Moving so his mouth was over her ear he whispered. "Did you reset the alarm when we came in the house?"

She nodded.

"Get dressed and lock yourself in the bathroom or closet. Do you have a weapon in here?" He was moving off the bed silently and pulling his jeans on. Looking out the window, the sun hadn't fully set, which made him wonder why an intruder hadn't waited until the cover of darkness.

Jaqui pulled a pair of leggings on and a T-shirt from her bag, but he didn't have time or want to alert the intruder to their whereabouts. Opening the case he'd had delivered by another SEAL team member, he pulled out a gun and handed one to Jaqui, then lifted the strap of the automatic weapon over his chest and palmed the Glock.

Padding silently to the closed door, he pressed his ear to the door. A cool hand at his back made him close his eyes in resignation.

He put his lips close to her ear and bit out. "Stay behind me."

As quietly as possible, he opened the door. The noise he'd heard was coming from the front of the house. He raised his brows at the off tune singing. A rendition of Adele's song Hello, was being belted out by a female that had Jaqui's eyes widening. Then he heard another voice chime in.

Jaqui started to laugh and tucked the gun into the back of her pants. "That would be my cousins. Annette and Maureen, or Nettie and Mo to those close to them. They're twins, and crazy as all get out. They're my Aunt Laci's girls."

Tay lifted his finger to his ear when the two women hit, or tried to hit a particular high note. "Do they think they can sing?"

The woman he loved with all his heart nudged him in the stomach. "Hush, you'll hurt their feelings."

He wasn't sure what he expected, but figured carrying around an assault rifle would scare the piss out of two young girls. "Give me a second while I put this away." He walked back into the bedroom, placing the gun back into the case and shutting it up, then bent and picked up his T-shirt.

He exhaled, and resigned himself to dealing with a couple of young girls.

However, the scene he walked into was nothing like he'd expected. First of all, the two young girls, were not the young girls he'd thought. They appeared to be closer to Jaqui's age. He rubbed his eyes, sure he was seeing double.

"Oh, he has that deer in the headlights look, Mo. I don't think Jaq told him we were identical. FYI, big boy, we don't go for that sort of thing." One of the women spoke in a slow southern-ish drawl.

"Ignore Nettie. Ever since she moved to Georgia and started dating Shep Calhoun of the *Calhoun's* of the south, sugar, she has started talking like that." The one he assumed was Mo made the man's name sound like a disease rather than a family.

Nettie stepped up to her sister. "Why, you're just upset I found me a man finer than a frog's hair."

Mo rolled her eyes. "See? What the flying fuck does that even mean?"

At this point his woman had a large glass of something fruity up to her lips, trying to keep from laughing, while he was thinking of ways he could escape.

"I'll have you know that means he is fine as fuck, in your gauche terms." Nettie fluffed up her strawberry blonde hair.

"Oh, that's rich. Aren't you the one who told me he said, and I quote, 'fell for you after watching you suck the heads off of some crawfish?' Pretty sure that is not the words, or thoughts of some fine upstanding citizen, thank you very much." Mo fluffed her hair, the action almost comical.

Nettie shrugged. "He was just being honest. I believe that is a good trait to have in my future husband. Besides, we met at Traci's bar the Naughty Girls. Everyone who is anyone goes there."

"You're lucky I love you like a sister, or I'd have you committed." Mo raised her half empty glass. "Are you just gonna stand there and gape, or introduce yourself?"

Tay looked from three sets of blue eyes, back to the only pair that held him. "Hello, ladies. I think I'll just go check my emails while you three talk." Or whatever the hell they were doing. Not once had he saw a look of anger pass over either woman's face, and Jaqui seemed to take it all in like it was normal. First, being woke by two females singing, or rather killing a great song, then this banter, he was sure he might be the one who needed therapy.

"Nettie, Mo, leave Tay alone. Tay, these are my Aunt Laci's girls, Mo and Nettie," she laughed as Nettie flipped her the bird.

"You're only one year older than we are. I don't think you need to refer to us as girls, sugar." Nettie's voice dripped southern charm.

"Nettie, how long have you been living down in Georgia that you have picked up not only their terms, but that accent?" Jaqui asked, setting the glass down just as a fake piece of fruit was lobbed at her head.

"See, that is what I've been saying. Ever since she came home last week, it's been like that. Seriously! She actually said," Mo made air quotes. "Musta coulda." Her eyes rounded in mock horror.

"Do you think we need to take her to the doctor? Maybe she was abducted by one of those aliens she swore she saw back in high school," Jaqui said with a laugh.

"Now, you listen. Don't be thinking yer too big for yer britches. I can still take you down. Heck, last week at the Naughty Girls, I whipped the shit out of a chick." Nettie cracked her knuckles.

Laughing, Mo stepped between them. "I am so not helping you this time, Nettie. The last time she nearly broke my arm and your nose. Besides, you're the one who's gone batshit cray cray."

He watched as Nettie shrugged her shoulder. "I know there is life on other planets. I mean just look at him." She pointed at Tay. "Real men do not look like that."

"Hey, eyes off him. He's not on the menu for either of you heifers," Jaqui goaded her cousins.

"Oh, no you didn't just call us that. Hold my earrings, sissy." Mo pretended to take off said jewelry.

"Well, since I have a party to go to at the country club when I go home with Shep, I guess I shouldn't teach you a lesson in manners. But, just so you know, I can see you're sweating like a stripper on Sunday." Nettie ducked the fruit Jaqui lobbed back at her.

Yeah, he was sure he had a concussion, or he'd stepped into an episode of Punk'd or something.

"Poor man. He has the look." Nettie wound her arm through Jaqui's. "Wait till I introduce him to Traci. Traci is somewhat sane. I mean she only shot her ex with a shotgun, but the shell was filled with toilet paper or something like that so they didn't charge her. I mean it was his fault for having that skank in her bed."

The woman of his dreams had the nerve to give him a little wave. "Girls, I think you're scaring poor Tay."

"Why don't I give y'all a chance to…um, talk." He began backing away. If he was asked, he would not admit it, but seeing Jaqui's twin cousins and their antics scared him a little. He was used to her no nonsense attitude. Tay wasn't sure how to react to the way the other two looked him up and down like he was a side of beef. Not to mention their easy banter, which he wasn't sure if they were serious, or not. Grabbing his computer from Jaqui's room, he headed back toward the big open living area, or the room he would call the front room. Hell, they probably called it something fancy.

"I'm sorry about them. My aunt told them we were here, and of course, they had to come and meet you." Her soft expression showed her love for the crazy duo.

Holding out his arm, he motioned her forward. "I think they're…adorable. Besides, they're your family. One small question though," he paused, looking around. "They don't seriously think they can sing do they?"

She burst out laughing, dispelling the anxiety he'd seen as she stepped into the hall leading from her suite of rooms. "If you ask them, they think they sing just like their favorite singers." She held up a finger for each artist. "From Adele, to Miranda Lambert, to Tim McGraw." She paused for affect before continuing. "When they're drunk. However, the rest of us, even when drunk don't agree. The only blessing is that they never tried out for American Idol, and I don't think they have plans for The Voice."

From the honesty in her gaze he was about to ask if that was the truth, but stopped himself. "Go have some fun with your cousins. I'm going to check in with Kai, and go over some emails." In reality he was going to hack their security and change the codes. No way in hell did he want to wake up to more caterwauling from the twins, let alone anyone else

227

who had access to the property. He'd wait until the other women left before he let Jaqui know.

Still, something nagged at him. Hope? Surely, but a worry and fear that it would all be snatched away made him sweat. He'd never truly loved anyone other than his parents and his SEAL team. Yeah, they may fight like brothers, because in a sense they were, but he knew they could take care of themselves. At the end of the day, any one of them could be taken out on a mission. It was a fact they each knew, but with their training and the fact they had each other's back, he never really thought of it when he was on a mission. Sighing, he pulled open his emails, automatically deleting over half a dozen before his eyes fell on one that caught his eye.

Clicking on the ominous looking email, he read the message, then re-read it to make sure he was reading it correctly. "Fuck," he swore, looking around for his cell, then realized he must've left it in Jaqui's room. Swiftly, he forwarded the message to Kai and his commander with a note he was calling in two minutes. Knowing Kai, he'd have his phone on him with the email notifications turned off.

He hurried back down the hall, making sure not to make any noise and alert Jaqui or the others. The devastating email would rock all their worlds. Inside the bedroom, he looked at the wrecked bed, and then his suitcase. Finally, his eyes fell on the floor next to the bed where he'd dropped his jeans earlier. The sound of the door opening behind him, had him drawing his gun automatically, only to exhale as Jaqui came in with a smile on her face. After putting the weapon back in place, he advanced on her.

"Holy shit, Tay, sorry I scared you." She raised her hands up in the air.

When he stayed quiet too long, she tilted her head to the side. "What's wrong? You're scaring me," she whispered.

"I got an email from an organization called Nameless. You've heard of them, right?" At her nod he continued. "They aren't naming names, but someone close to our team has been leaking information to Medellin, and even gave them your parents' name and address. I'm sorry, baby." The words came out in a rush before he could stop them.

A tear slipped down her cheek. "So, my parents' accident wasn't an accident, but a hit?"

He grabbed her, holding her like the anchor he hoped she wanted him to be. "I've got a call into Kai and the commander. We will have protection on them at the hospital and here." The promise made his words harsher than he'd planned.

Tay closed his eyes and rested his forehead against hers. Hearing her suck her breath in, he fought the urge to ship her back to Hawaii where she'd be surrounded by the Navy. His entire being shook with the force of the need to protect.

"We need to get my cousins out of here. More than likely they are watching this house. How are we going to protect them, too?" Jaqui pushed away from him, and he let her go.

Bitterness tinged her voice. She'd suffered at the cartel's hands. Knew firsthand what happened and barely survived with her life.

"We'll take them with us to the hospital and explain the danger they're in. By then I should have some reinforcements." He brushed his thumb over her bottom lip, hating the worry on her face.

She wiped her palms on her thighs, straightened her shoulders, and stood straight. "Okay, let's do this."

If he hadn't already loved her, he would have fallen head over ass in that moment.

# Chapter Ten

She automatically wanted to stand behind Tay and let him take the lead. Years of training kicked in. Yes, she'd been tortured. But, she survived, and she would not allow Jose Medellin and the Bloque Cartel to take anything or anyone else from her. Especially not her family. The borrowed gun Tay gave her was secured in her purse. How she wished she had her own weapons, and the holsters she was comfortable with. Looking over as he drove them back toward the hospital, his white knuckle grip on the steering wheel didn't make the butterflies in her stomach any easier.

"Okay, so are you going to explain why we couldn't drive ourselves to the hospital, or keep us in suspense?" Mo's exasperated voice belied the tension in her cousin's tone. Jaqui wondered if the family had been filled in on her injuries while in Columbia by her mother.

Jaqui turned to face Mo and Nettie, wanting, needing them to see the honesty in her expression. "I need for you to trust Tay and I. As soon as we get to the hospital we will explain everything to everyone at the same time. But, this is a huge deal. Both of you need to promise not to leave our sides until after we have explained. Promise me." Jaqui met two pairs of blue eyes in the backseat of their rental car. Damn, she wished they had a military grade rig that was bulletproof. With the new information, driving through the streets of Vegas, she felt like a bullseye was drawn on them.

Nettie nodded. "I want to go home. Shep would send a plane for me in a heartbeat. Is that possible?" The southern accent she'd had since Jaqui had walked into her parents' kitchen was gone.

She automatically shook her head, reaching back to take Nettie's hand. "Not yet. I know you think you'd be safe with him or in your own home, but we just don't know. I'm sorry I brought this here."

"Bullshit," Tay snarled.

Jaqui turned to stare at him. "What?"

Tay glanced her way, then back at the road. "This is not your fault. Don't apologize to them or anyone

233

again. You didn't do shit except get kidnapped, beaten, and nearly die at the hands of a fucking madman, so don't fucking apologize. You survived. Don't let me hear you say you're sorry for that again or I'll turn your ass over my damn knee and spank you."

Gasps echoed from the back, but Jaqui couldn't tear her eyes away from the man she loved and knew he loved her just as fiercely. "You're right. It's not my fault."

"Damn right it's not." He grabbed her hand and brought it to his lips. The tingle of awareness went straight to her heart. She sucked in a breath of air, savoring the light caress.

A nagging feeling that they were running out of time hit her. She catalogued every detail as they entered the hospital, knowing Tay did the same. Her cousins, the laughing women from earlier no longer laughed, instead they were wary and stayed close, looking at each person they passed as a threat. God, she hated that she'd brought her shit to them. No matter that she hadn't done it on purpose.

Luckily, her parents had been moved to a private room and with the amount of pull they'd had, were able to get both beds in the same area. However, they were unable to be put in the same room due to the difference in their injuries, and the amount of machines her mother still required. They stopped in to see her dad first, his demeanor much more aware, yet the strain of the move and surgery showed.

"Hi, Dad. You look like you're ready to jump out the window, or rip the IV out any moment." She kissed his cheek.

His eyes looked past her and landed on Mo and Nettie then Tay. "Why are you all looking so somber? Is your mother okay? Laci said they'd moved her just down the hall." He attempted to pull the blanket off, his voice rising.

Jaqui put her hand over his, stilling his movements. "First off, mom is fine. Second, we came here to speak with you first. I have some news that will impact all of us." She took a deep breath, then looked over for Tay's support. His nod of encouragement gave her the strength to go on. After she explained what she could about Columbia, and how it now impacted her family, she could see the worry etching his fifty-one year old face.

"Is your mother safe here in the hospital?" He asked gruffly.

"Sir, the Navy is sending personnel to protect you both. Every employee will be thoroughly checked before they are allowed entrance into either of your rooms. We will do all we can, but until we have eliminated the threat, we need you to take extra precautions as well."

Her dad narrowed his eyes. "Son, I can assure you I'll do my damndest. What're you doing to protect my baby?"

To give Tay credit, he didn't squirm under her dad's direct gaze or question. Most men, or boys in her past had never been able to handle his gruff attitude.

"Believe me, sir. I will protect her with my last breath."

If it came to it, she'd do the same for him.

"Good enough. Now, what about my other girls?" Her dad pointed to his nieces standing far too quietly by the door.

Nettie was the first to speak up. "I want to go home to Shep but he says it's not safe."

"We'll do whatever we're told, Uncle Lance. I have a confession to make that nobody, or at least not many people know about. I was actually going to tell my parents this weekend." Mo looked nervous. "I've been dating the owner of one of the largest casinos here in Vegas for a while now. He's sort of asked me to marry him." She flashed a guilty look at her twin sister.

"What," Nettie squealed.

Mo smiled. "My point is, nobody knows and he is very rich and has lots of bodyguards. I could easily secure a suite for us in his hotel with none the wiser. Believe me, you can't get in the elevator to his area unless you have the proper access. Jose whoever wouldn't be able to get in there."

Tay asked which casino. Jaqui couldn't help but smile as she heard.

"What do you think, Tay?" Jaqui looked at her lover.

"Let me clear it with Kai and the Commander. We need to fill your aunt and uncle in, but I don't think it's wise to tell your mom in her present condition," Tay spoke with conviction, looking at Lance for confirmation.

Lance Wallace nodded in agreement. "My wife has suffered enough already. The last thing she needs to find out is that our baby," he stopped and choked up. "That's the last thing a parent ever needs to know, especially when you can't hold her properly." He held his arms out.

Jaqui went into them willingly. Her dad's arms were always a place she felt safe, yet now she had Tay. She let her father hold her a few moments, loving his fatherly embrace and knowing he'd always be there for her. "I love you, daddy."

"Love you too, baby girl."

When she'd finally realized Tay wasn't coming back, she'd wanted to rush home and let her parents do what they'd always done, and that was hold her and make her feel better. At the time she'd decided big girls didn't need to run home and cry to mommy and daddy. It wasn't until six weeks later, when she'd missed a period, her life had turned upside down. She'd been frightened. Scared. When she thought of having a baby, every emotion had ran the gamut, but then she'd come to the conclusion she'd love to be pregnant. At ten weeks, she'd worked up the courage to call Tay, had it planned out in her head even though he'd avoided her like the plague, when she'd woken in the middle of the night with the worst cramps she'd ever had. She'd stumbled to the restroom only to find herself bleeding. She'd called her mother from Hawaii crying. They'd wanted to rush to her side, but by the time they got there it would've been too late.

A shiver wracked her frame at the memory of the loss. Yes, they'd used protection, but somehow, whether the condom had leaked, or what, she'd gotten pregnant, and then lost their baby.

Her dad held her away from him, but she shook her head. He'd wanted to track Tay down and beat the

239

shit out of him then, but she'd told them he had no clue she was pregnant. Now, looking at him, she tried to convey that she still hadn't told Tay about the loss.

"You have some explaining to do, girl. You know things tend to come out when you don't want them to. It's always best they come from us, than someone else," her father warned.

Yeah, she knew that. She couldn't bring herself to tell Tay yet. What difference would it make in the long run? "I will, promise." There was a lot she needed to do and think about, but right now protecting her family was more important than something that couldn't be fixed or changed.

**\*\*\*\***

Tay watched the exchange between father and daughter, and knew he was missing something. Lance Wallace was warning Jaqui, his words made her body stiffen, and he didn't like it one bit.

A brisk knock on the door kept him from demanding answers. Nettie and Mo both jumped like cats on a hot tin roof. A fact he hated, especially when he'd witnessed the fun, easy going women from earlier.

Two soldiers stood at the entrance and saluted him as he approached, their military attire and stance made them appear official. However, Tay wasn't taking anything at face value. "Credentials, men." Yeah, he outranked them and wasn't above using it. They gave him the code word they'd been given. He nodded, then looked back at the others in the room. "One will be stationed outside of your dad's room, while another outside your mother's. They will have twenty-four hour protection, and a new code will be selected for each change. It's the best we can do right now. As for the staff at the hospital, the commander is handling the background checks, and making sure each man guarding your mom and dad has a list of who can, and can't enter. That includes the nurses and doctors on staff. If someone calls in, and a replacement is in place, there is going to be a hiccup that will no doubt create issues. Again, nothing is foolproof, but we will do the best we can. Our best bet is to have someone we trust with each of your parents."

"My aunt doesn't want to leave my mom, but I don't think Dave will want her here once he finds out the danger." Jaqui chewed her lip.

Mo stepped forward. "It's probably safer for her to be here, than their sprawling ranch outside of the city limits. I'll just point that out. As for my dad, he's going to be the one we need to worry about. He thinks he's all big and bad."

Nettie sniffed. "Oh, he'll listen if I have to hogtie his ass."

The girls laughed at her southern accent and words.

"There's my new hillbilly sister." Mo wrapped her arm around Nettie.

Tay led the way toward the other hospital room. Glances cast their way made him swear beneath his breath as they headed into the wing where Maci was. He hoped like hell the staff didn't go around running their mouths about the security that was now in place. He could see Jose and his men coming in like a tornado ripping through, destroying everything in its path.

Jaqui eased inside the door, making sure she didn't open it wide enough for the occupants to see the military personnel now stationed outside. Although it was for all their protection, she agreed the less stress on Maci the better. Moments later Laci and Dave came out, leaving Jaqui inside with her mom.

Laci was quick to embrace her daughters, while Dave, the man the twins had said would be the bull in the family stayed back, eyeing him.

"Alright, son, explain," Dave said, suspicion laced his deep rumble.

The clearly perceptive uncle was no dummy, yet he knew the man was going to put up a fight.

He led them all over to the visitors' area, making sure they were alone before he explained what he could. Each minute away from Jaqui felt like hours. He kept staring toward the area where Maci's room was. Although he'd left her with the soldier outside keeping guard, he wouldn't relax until she was next to him.

Dave rubbed the back of his neck. "So, what you're saying is we're safest here? But, for how long? It's not like we can eat, sleep and shower. Do all the normal things here forever." Dave paced away.

"Not forever, no. Lance will be released before Maci. I know it's not ideal, but until we can get more intel on Medellin, or neutralize the threat, it's the best we can do for right now." Fire burned in his gut at the truth of his statement. Damn, he wished to hell Medellin would have died in Columbia.

"We can stay at Alan's hotel. He has security the president would envy," Mo interjected.

Tay wanted to tell her the cartel could get to them there, but didn't want to scare her. Hell, the hotel was probably a lot safer than the hospital. "Use my secure line and you can call him. You can't tell him exactly what is going on, but tell him it's a matter of safety, and if he needs to speak to me, I'll give him the version I am able to."

Fear stamped the women's faces, except for Jaqui who walked out of her mother's room and heard the last of his words. God, he loved her.

They gave Mo a little room for privacy while she placed her call. A few minutes later she came back with a small smile on her face. "He's flying out tonight, but has given me access to his suite on the top floor. Nobody else will be able to get up there except Alan, and those with me, he's assured me."

Nodding, he took his phone back. "Good. We'll take you over and escort you up." He pulled Jaqui to his side, brushing a kiss to brow. "You ready to go, or do you want to stay and visit with your parents?" His dominating side was definitely pushing to the front of his psyche, but there was nothing else he could do but try to control what was in his power.

"No, she's sleeping. Let's get these two over to the casino, then can we stop back by here on our way back?" Oh, yeah. His woman was fire and ice. Her eyes dared him to deny her, yet her body braced for his denial.

"Mr. Hyland, you okay with staying or do you want to go with us?" He didn't allow Jaqui to see the twitch in his lips, and hoped like hell nobody noticed his arousal.

Dave looked at his girls. "You think they'll be safe there?"

Tay had already made the necessary texts to Kai, who he knew was already getting men in place, or at least organizing it at the casino. Alan Mancini owned one of the premier casinos on the strip and if Tay knew anything, the man had to have some major security set up. Problem was, he didn't know the man himself. Once they were back at Jaqui's parents' home, he'd do some checking, and see if he couldn't hack the security himself. If he couldn't then it was secure. If he could hack it…well depending on how easy it was to get in made all the difference.

"I'm not going to lie, sir, but they will be safer there than here." He gave the honest answer and waited.

The air seemed to hang while they all waited. Although he knew the twins were a year or two younger than Jaqui, they were still this man's children. "That's better than I expected." He held his arms out, and both girls surged into his brawny arms.

Tay and Jaqui gave them a little space, watching as people went about the halls. The soldier stationed outside of Maci's door stood straight, eyes and body transmitted a confidence that he'd kick anyone's ass who dared try and enter.

"Alright, let's get this show on the road," Nettie said with a sigh.

"Have you told Shep anything yet?" Jaqui asked as they made their way back to the bank of elevators.

Nettie groaned. "Damn it, no. What am I supposed to tell him? Hey, baby, you know how I went to visit my family? Well, guess what...there's this madman drug kingpin fella who wants to off my cousin. Oh, yeah, and just because I'm related, he might do me in too. Love you, bye Felicia." Her snarky comment made them all laugh, especially the last words said in such a tone that was completely devoid of a southern accent.

Walking out, the trio of women looked almost like triplets, except Jaqui's hair was a little blonder, and longer. With the heat of Vegas though they all had their hair up in messy buns that he couldn't wait to take down and run his hands through. "I bet you three were terrors growing up together," he mused as he unlocked the vehicle after making sure it was safe.

Jaqui giggled. "You have no clue what they would put me up to. Heck, I was older by a year than these two hellions, yet you'd think they were the older ones. I think it was the power of the twins that did it."

"Can I ride up front? I tend to get a little car sick if I already have an upset stomach, and I'm afraid this afternoon has made my stomach all kinds of queasy." Nettie held a palm against her abdomen.

Tay glanced at the younger woman, worry creased his brow. "Are you okay? You're not pregnant are you?"

He heard Jaqui suck in a breath, but opened the passenger door for Nettie and looked at Jaqui to make sure it was okay. Her nod reassured him.

"Oh god no. Seriously, I just get a little anxiety that shows up in nausea. Yay me. Not!"

After making sure all the women were in the vehicle, he got in, looking in the rearview mirror, he saw the uncertainty in Jaqui. There was nothing he could do at the moment other than get the two Hyland women to their safe location.

At the casino, he hated leaving his SUV for valet, but Mo assured him it would be safe. Of course, he'd go over it with the bomb searching device before they left. A thought struck him, and he made a quick decision to switch vehicles before leaving. He grabbed his pack and Jaqui's, shouldering them before circling around. They'd agreed to not speak to anyone, which apparently was a common thing for Mo when she came with Alan. Dressed as they were, they didn't draw a lot of attention. He walked behind the women, eyes and ears open as much as possible. The constant sounds of slot machines and people calling out kept him on edge, until they made it to the private lift. A large man stood in front of it, his expensive suit clearly hand tailored to fit him.

"Excuse me, I have access to the penthouse," Mo said with a haughty tone he'd never heard from her.

"Of course, ma'am. I'm told you have the code." He moved to the side giving access to a keypad. Once Mo moved in front of it, the bodyguard placed his own body behind, keeping anyone else from seeing what she entered.

"Thank you...um, I'm sorry, I don't know your name." Mo's cheeks turned pink.

"Reece, ma'am." He looked Tay up and down. "Mr. Mancini said you and your sister were the only ones staying.

Mo nodded. "Yeah, they're just going to come up and make sure it's all clear."

It was past time for him to show the big man he was not some lightweight to be dismissed. "Thanks, Reece. I got it from here." Tay ushered the women inside, not missing the clear sign of a gun holstered at the back of Reece's waist, or the way the man's hand flexed. Tay rethought his plan of waiting until they got back to Jaqui's place to research Alan and his casino. Knowledge was power.

Reece didn't look back at them as the elevator shut silently. The long flight up, Tay waited for the thing to come to a halt and for men to come pouring in, exhaling a sigh of relief as the doors opened on the top floor. They stepped out and a large foyer greeted them with another set of double doors and a keypad.

"Extra security in case someone somehow got past the first one," Mo explained. This time she wasn't as cautious entering the code since it was just the four of them, and Tay watched the numbers, memorizing them automatically. He nearly laughed as he watched her punch in the numbers eight, six, seven, five, three, zero, and nine. The song about a girl named Jenny by Tommy Tutone.

To say the place was grand would be a major understatement. He'd seen shows where rock stars and the like had parties, and clips from scenes at suites in Vegas, yet none of them compared to what they stepped in to.

"Damn, girl. You done did good for yourself. I'm guessing it would be silly to ask him what kind of ground clearance his truck has," Nettie joked, looking shell shocked.

Mo stared around as if seeing it for the first time. "It's nice, but I've only been here a couple times. Come on, we can sleep in one of the guest rooms."

Tay wondered why they weren't going to sleep in the master suite. "You ladies mind if I look around and check out the security?"

"That would be wonderful." Mo looked scared. Nettie not as sickly as she'd been when they'd left the hospital.

It took him a solid twenty minutes to complete his inspection, satisfied with the security for the most part. Someone would have to land on the roof and rappel down. Not that the cartel didn't have that ability, he just didn't see them putting that much effort into getting to two cousins. He checked in on Jaqui and saw they were in deep conversation. The need to verify Alan was a good man, and on the up and up consumed him.

A half hour later, Tay sat back stunned. Alan looked like the debonair business man that he presented to the world. Rich, good looking, and a ladies' man. However, Tay wondered what the man would do when he found out someone had been recording his comings and goings, piggybacking on his own security cameras. Fuck! He scrubbed his hand down his face, looking toward the area he could hear Jaqui and the twins coming from. He wondered how much Mo loved the man, and figured he'd wait to break her heart until after he could get them out of the man's hotel. He'd scrubbed the security camera in the elevator where someone had hacked and recorded. Tay wasn't sure how long they'd been recording, and what all they'd seen, but he'd make damn sure the last bit was never seen by anyone.

Worry made him look again toward where the women were. If Alan knew his secret was out, would he kick Mo and Nettie to the curb? Hell, Tay would make damn sure the man understood the U.S. Government didn't take kindly to men who would be so callous to another human, let alone one who was considered under their protection. Overstepping boundaries? Sure, but he didn't give a shit.

"Does it pass muster, Tay?" Mo came in with a glass flute filled with golden liquid.

He shut down his computer and stood. "I made a few adjustments to his security cameras. Nothing he'll notice, but tell him to give me a call when you speak with him." His mind made up, he gave Mo his number.

"At least we are getting to relax in the lap of luxury. I mean, we have our own private pool and everything."

Tay had seen all that, too. On the top level there were no other suites and the big man at the bottom kept everyone out. He hoped if someone was trailing them, they'd see the impossibility and choose an easier target.

The feel of his phone buzzing had him holding his finger up. "Excuse me, ladies, it's Kai."

# Chapter Eleven

Tay went outside for some privacy to talk with Kai. He'd sent the information he'd gotten on Alan to him, knowing they may need it.

"Damn, Tay. Warn a brother before you send shit like that." Kai's growl was almost as bad as his bite.

"You don't like porn?" Tay joked.

"You can't see me right now, but I'm flipping you off. Hang on, cause I'm giving you two middle fingers, fucker."

The sound of jets or planes alerted him that Kai was on his way. His next words confirmed his suspicions.

"We just landed in Vegas. I have a few things to clear, then we'll rendezvous at Jaqui's. I brought your stuff."

By stuff, Kai meant Tay's own weapons, along with Jaqui's he was sure. They didn't fly commercial while on a mission, and this was officially a mission. A fact he hadn't informed Jaqui of yet. Shit! "Can you send a pickup for Jaqui and me? I don't trust the car now that it's been in the hands of god knows how many people."

"That makes sense. Yeah, let me do some maneuvering. I can have Oz there in twenty minutes. Text when you are at the front and he'll tell you what he's in."

"Thanks, Kai. See you at Jaqui's parents."

Kai gave him his arrival time. Tay was glad it wouldn't be just him guarding Jaqui any longer.

"See you then. I'm assuming you have the entire team with you?"

"I won't even answer that dumb ass question as I'm assuming you've got shit for brains, since you landed in Vegas and all. Must be the dry air or some shit." Kai disconnected before Tay could reply.

He laughed as he pocketed the phone. Kai was one hundred percent in love with Hawaii. Oh, the man could adapt anywhere, but hearing him blame the air on Tay's question made him laugh out loud.

"What are you laughing about?" Jaqui asked, coming up behind him to wrap her arms around his waist. Having her close always settled him. He should have realized she had done that for him even back before they'd made love. His heart, mind and body was now of one accord. Jaqui Wallace was it for him. He was exactly what Kai had called him, only not because of the dry air, but because he'd let the best thing that had ever happened to him slip away. Or rather, he'd ran like a little bitch. Well, he was done running, unless it was for Jaqui, then he would always run for her.

"You really do freak me out when you go all silent Bob on me." Jaqui ran her fingers over his close cropped hair, pulling his head down for a deep searing kiss.

He pulled her close, kissing her back just as frantic to claim her mouth.

A cough interrupted them, followed by the loud clearing of a throat.

"Yo, no banging of my cuz on the patio in broad daylight, handsome." Mo stood with her hands on slim hips.

"It's her fault. She kissed me first." Tay held a squirming Jaqui in front of him, hiding the erection tenting his pants. At the rate he was going, he would have a zipper indent permanently scarring his cock.

Nettie pointed at them. "You're the one with your hands on her ass, big guy. Come on, I'm hungry, Mo. Let's order room service. Do you think that handsome guy downstairs will deliver it to us?"

"Aren't you engaged to one Shep Calhoun of the Calhoun's?" Mo glared at her twin.

"Hey, I may be engaged, but I ain't dead. Did you see that man's guns?" Nettie held her hands above her own biceps.

"Ladies, I don't think it's wise to mess with that man. Now, if you order delivery, how does it get delivered?" Tay worried his bottom lip.

Mo shrugged. "There are several restaurants on site. Usually I just order and someone delivers it."

Damn. He hadn't thought of that complication. "I'll speak with Reece, but you two do not leave the suite, and don't let anyone in. Promise me."

They both agreed, then he and Jaqui were making their way back down. He verified the delivery of food would go through Reece, and that it was done via computer ordering so nobody would know who was in the suite. Tay figured it was as good as he could make it, and left with a nod to the bodyguard. Before they went back to valet to get the SUV, he tugged Jaqui into a packed bar and grill.

"Are you hungry, too?" She asked looking around.

Bending close he explained about switching the cars and that Oz was picking them up. Her eyes widened. Relief washed over her features. "What about the twins? Is there going to be extra security on them?"

Tay was pretty sure there was more than just Reece watching, especially since this was a drug trafficking case with possible connections on U.S. soil. Other agencies than just he and his team had interests in the cartel. However, he didn't want to freak Jaqui out.

"I'm sure there are more than just that hulk guarding them, not to mention, it'll take more than a casual stroll to reach that suite. You and I are going to make sure they see us leave, but we're not going to get into a vehicle that could've been compromised." Tay spoke only the truth, knowing she'd see a lie.

As she stared him in the eye, he held his breath. Her nod of acceptance eased his fears slightly. Still, he had a knowing sense of doom he couldn't shake.

"Let's do this and get it over with." Jaqui chewed her bottom lip as she pulled away.

He tenderly tucked her into his side. "Stay next to me, sunshine. I know you can take care of yourself, but humor me."

\*\*\*\*

Fear and love stole all the oxygen from her lungs. The man was truly one in a million, and she wasn't sure if she was worthy. It took all her resolve to allow

Tay to take the lead, knowing he would also take a bullet for her. Jose Medellin might keep her alive to play with her, but he'd kill Tay and any other man on principle. She knew he'd want to get her back in order to make an example of her. What that example would be is a mystery, but she had no doubt it would be full of pain and humiliation. Shivers wracked her at the thoughts swirling around her head.

The closer they got to the entrance, the more she became aware of her surroundings. Every person around her became a threat in her mind. It would be all too easy for one of the kingpin's thugs to open fire, killing anyone who stepped in his way. However, that wouldn't make the bastard feel as though he'd gotten his revenge, and everyone knew he wanted payback. Now, they were waiting for him to make his next move since he'd made sure she was in Vegas, instead of safely tucked away in Hawaii where she was surrounded by military personnel.

Stepping outside, the bright sun blinded her for a minute and she closed her eyes against the sunlight, giving her a chance to adjust. "Damn it. I must've left my sunglasses up in the suite."

Tay squeezed her hand. "Oz is here." He pointed at a large SUV that looked nothing like the one they'd rented pulling up with tinted windows.

"How do you know that's Oz?" She eased back, sucking in a deep breath of hot humid air.

He showed her the screen of his phone with an image of Oz next to the vehicle, then one of the man sitting inside flipping Tay the bird. "The man is insane."

"Wasn't it you and he who jumped out of a perfectly good airplane?" Tay's low growled words had her stopping before she reached the vehicle.

"Well, yeah, but that was because he dared me to." She wasn't sure why he was freaking out over something she and Oz had done a couple years back. Heck, she loved extreme sports of all kinds. Well, she was marking off running with the bulls even though it hadn't officially been on her list of things to do before she died.

Tay opened the back door, glaring at her while she climbed in. She waited for him to climb into the front beside Oz, then he turned around. "So, you do whatever someone dares you?" Heat flared in his blue eyes. "Well yeehaw, sunshine. I'll be sure to remember that little factoid."

Oh, she wasn't sure she liked the way he said those words, nor the gleam in his eyes. "Of course not. I mean I love to skydive, Tay."

Again, she didn't understand his anger.

"Skydiving is where you have a chute. You and jackass here jumped out of a plane with nothing." He jerked his thumb toward Oz.

"Hey, we were over a large body of water," Oz laughed.

"Shut it, Oz. I still don't understand why the hell you dared her in the first place." Tay turned to face the front, flipping the visor down so he could meet Jaqui's eyes.

Oz shrugged his big shoulders. "At the time, I thought it would be a great ice breaker."

Jaqui really needed to get the conversation off of that time. She'd turned Oz down because she'd had a thing for Tay. She'd just been too scared at the time to admit it to him or anyone how she felt. It was shortly after that she'd decided it was time to reach out and take what she wanted. Which wasn't Oz, although the man was sex on a stick, he wasn't it for her.

"What's the plan?" She hated the idea they needed one, but better to be proactive, than blindsided.

Oz and Tay exchanged glances.

"Excuse me assholes, but I am part of the team. Remember, I'm the one he kidnapped and beat. I'm the one whose parents were targeted. Don't fucking think to leave me out." She got louder with each word.

"Is that what you think we're doing?" Tay turned in his seat.

"Clearly. I mean look at you both. Do you not think I can see he was checking with you before he answered? I'm far from stupid, Tay." She could tell her words angered him.

"Do you have any idea what kind of hell I faced when I saw you lying beneath that jaguar?" he demanded. "I have fucked up so many times in my life, but none so much as with you. I never want to face that same deep fear as I did back in Columbia." There was so much feeling reflected in his tone and features, she wanted to reach out and reassure him she'd never put him through that again. However, they were both in the Navy and couldn't make promises like that.

She swallowed the instant denial. "Tay, I would never intentionally put myself in the hands of a madman, or in danger. You know that some things can't be prevented. Like the fact you and I are both in professions that put us in danger occasionally." Granted, she'd never thought to be in the position she'd been.

Tay reached back, his large tan hand had a slight tremor. "I know, and that kills me."

"So help me. Don't keep me in the dark and make me an easy target," her voice came out a choked whisper.

"I love you, Jaqui. I'll do my best." His voice came out a deep growl, sending a shiver down her spine.

"That's all I ask." Hating the wobble, she squeezed his fingers before letting go.

Oz drove them to her parents place without asking for directions, amazing her since she didn't think he knew where they lived. The man must've gotten the info on the way from Hawaii. Sometimes she was a little scared at the information the SEALs could get, and memorize in a short amount of time. It hit home again why she was not cut out to be one.

Another military issue vehicle sat in the circle drive, looking completely out of place. "Boys and their toys," she mumbled, hopping out without thought for her safety.

"Damn it, Jaqui. Why can't you wait for me to open your door?"

She rolled her eyes. "You mean shield me with your body?"

"She's got you there, cowboy." Oz tossed the keys in the air as he strolled to the door.

"Shut up," Tay barked and moved her forward with a big hand at her back. Her world had been turned upside down in the last few months, if not the last two years. She put her hand on her stomach, the loss hit her again.

"Are you sick?" Tay looked at her face and where she rested her hand, concern written on his face.

"Oh, no. I'm fine. Well, as fine as someone who is being stalked by a psycho drug dealer." She added a little laugh to make it sound like a joke. In truth her stomach was churning.

They walked inside to find the rest of Tay's team in her parents' kitchen. Kai stood as they entered.

"Hey, how are your mom and dad?" She could see the concern on Kai's face.

She filled them in on the latest update for both parents, then heaved a heavy sigh. "Alright, what's the plan?"

Again, the men looked to Tay before answering her. She tapped her foot, seriously thinking of ways to throat punch each and every one of them simultaneously.

"She's got that look, boss," Coyle spoke up.

Sully nodded. "Just so you know, I think you can totally handle it."

Tay scowled at the two men. "Where did you two's balls go?" He looked around the room.

Sully grabbed his crotch. "I know exactly where my balls are, and I don't have any designs to have a pint sized dynamo kick them into my throat."

"Hey, I only did that on accident, Sully." Jaqui walked over to the gorgeous man with piercing green eyes. With his mixed heritage, he had the best of both worlds. A gorgeous complexion, full lips that made women drool, and eyes that were a shade of green she'd only seen in movies. And, he was a flirt of the worst kind. They'd ran into each other at a nightclub in Honolulu. Never one to actually go out much, she'd let her hair down and drank a little too much. When a man had cornered her near the ladies' room, she had tried to get away, only to run into another solid form. Her fight instinct had kicked in, making her knee the unknown assailant. Only it had been Sully coming to her rescue when he'd realized she'd drank too much.

"Why do I feel like everyone has secrets and stories with Jaqui?" Tay scowled at the room as if expecting them to admit he was correct.

Heat suffused her face. "Don't change the subject." She rounded the center island, opening the fridge the cool air felt good. Grabbing a bottle of water, she held it up for Tay to see. "Want a drink?"

"Yeah. Thanks." He came and took the bottle, pressing a quick kiss to her temple.

Jaqui sat down at the table and looked at the men surrounding her. Without the presence of her mom banging around, trying to create a meal for their guests, it felt wrong.

Half listening to the information they'd gathered, she realized her phone was in her bag and got up to check for messages. A gasp left her lips at the sight of several texts from Nettie.

"Shit," she whispered. Her hand shook as she called Nettie's cell. She felt the men in the room stand, the attention on her.

"Jaq, I think we're in trouble. When our order came up, Mo said that something seemed off. Now, I can't get her to wake up, and I'm scared." Nettie had tears in her voice.

"Is she breathing?"

A deep inhale could be heard through the line. "Yeah. And her heart seems to be beating normally. I think they put something in the food. I hadn't eaten anything yet. My stomach was in knots, and then Shep called, so I stepped outside to talk with him. When I came back in, she was slumped over on the couch. I'm scared, Jaqui."

She felt like every fear was exposed. First her parents, now her two beautiful cousins were targeted. All because of her.

"Hey, it's not your fault, baby." Tay told her then took the phone, pressing the speaker button.

"Have you alerted Reece that something was wrong?" Tay asked Nettie.

Nettie's whimper had Jaqui's heart breaking for the other woman. "I tried calling Jaqui first, and sent her a text. I was too scared to send him anything. He might be in on it."

"Good girl. You did the right thing. We're on our way. If something changes with Mo, and you feel you need to call an ambulance, do it," Kai said, his tone even. "Keep this line open and be sure to answer when I call back. Most importantly don't let anyone up there except me and Jaqui. Is there any place you can get you and your sister into that has a lock? Some place that will put an extra door or two between you and the elevator?"

Jaqui pictured Nettie frantically searching and then she remembered the tour. "Nettie, take her to Alan's room. I know for a fact his door had a huge deadbolt and it was open. Get in there, lock the door, and push a dresser in front of the door. Do it now."

271

Kai nodded.

The guys were standing, pulling on their weapons she had noticed lying next to them. Tay had a strained look.

"You want to order me to stay here, yet you don't feel it's safe. I see it written so clearly on your face. FYI, not gonna happen, big guy." She stood and held her hand out.

With reluctance he nodded, but didn't stop her as she rushed to get her own gun and ammo in place. She will gut the fucker if he so much as touches a hair on either one of her cousins.

They loaded up in the two vehicles. She sat in back of the one Oz had picked them up in with Tay up front, while Kai, Sully and Coyle drove the other. The speed they drove out of the gated community would probably make it into the monthly online paper, but she truly gave no fucks in that moment.

"Call and see if your cousin was able to do what you told her to do. I don't know how much or what drug the other one was given, but hopefully it wasn't too much and she will wake up soon." Kai navigated the roads like an expert.

As they came to a rocking stop at the entrance, all eyes turned toward them. Kai's commanding presence had the guy stepping up to tell them they couldn't park there, backing off with a look of awe on his face. "Touch either vehicle, and I'll have your ass thrown so far inside a cell, nobody will find you." The threat said in such a low tone had the hair on her nape standing up. Yeah, she totally understood why he was the one in charge.

Tay kept her between him and Coyle, Oz and Sully brought up the rear while Kai was in the lead. Inside the casino the patrons, for the most part, didn't pay the heavily armed individuals marching past hardly any attention. Clearly they had seen much weirder things.

At the bottom of the elevator, Jaqui expected to find the bear of a man Reece. What she found was an unmanned elevator, making her heart sink. "Reece should be here. We haven't been gone but an hour or so," she whispered loudly.

Kai pushed the button and then realized they needed a code. "Fuck, what's the code to get up?"

"Move," Jaqui shoved Kai out of the way and punched in the sequence.

"I don't even want to know." Tay nodded.

The doors slid open and each man had a gun aimed inside. Coyle was the first in, making sure it was safe before they entered.

"When the lift opens, I know the code there," Tay said.

Jaqui was glad since she hadn't gotten that one.

They rode up, tension mounting with every floor. The last call to Nettie had gone to voicemail. Of course, she knew it could be that her cousin's phone had died, or she was in the middle of getting them to safety. Or…she didn't want to think about the other options.

The door to the suite was open, a sinking feeling hit Jaqui at the knowledge they could be too late. She straightened her shoulders and nodded at the men.

Remnants of the dinner they had delivered was on the coffee table. She made a motion of her head and hands to show where the master suite was. She took a deep, silent breath, letting it out as they split up. Kai and Tay went toward the suite where Mo and Nettie should be, with her following on their heels, while Oz, Coyle and Sully fanned out to scout the rest of the rooms.

Kai tried the door, seeing the handle not turn she had a moment of triumph. Kai held his finger up, made a motion for them to back up, then attached a device to the locking mechanism. A small popping echoed around the hall and then there was a hole where the handle used to be. No scream or any noise at all came from the room.

"Shouldn't they be screaming or something?" Jaqui asked Tay's back.

Kai used a camera on the end of a pen inside the hole he created. "There is no movement in the room," he muttered.

Oz and Coyle came up to them. "Sully is guarding the door. We didn't find anyone in the apartment."

"Let's get this door open. Are you sure there was no other way in or out other than the elevator?" Kai looked her in the eyes.

Jaqui was breathing hard. "Mo said no."

Kai and Oz worked to push the door open. The dresser Nettie had shoved in front of it clearly doing a good job of keeping them out, or at least slowing them down.

Her mind blanked when they entered and she saw Mo lying so still on the floor. A whimper escaped her throat. Moving on legs not quite steady, she fell next to her cousin, hands shaking she brushed the strawberry blonde hair back from a warm forehead. "Oh god. She's alive."

"Get a medic," Tay ordered.

Oz was already dialing on his cell. She heard him telling them the situation, but couldn't let go of Mo's hand. "Where's Nettie?" She looked around the room.

Kai and Tay were checking every inch of space. The large master bath was bigger than her bedroom.

Mo's eyes fluttered open. "What's happened, Jaq?"

Knowing she had to stay strong, she looked up to catch a fleeting glance from Sully. He shook his head. "Is there another exit from the master room to the hotel?"

Licking her lips, Mo grabbed her head. "I think there's an emergency exit, but I've never used it."

"Where's it at?" Sully asked.

"The closet behind some suits. Why? What's happened?" She sat up, groaning, looking like she was in pain.

Jaqui helped her. "Someone drugged your food and took Nettie."

"This is your fault," Mo screamed, her hand came up and slapped Jaqui across the cheek.

The sound deafening, yet Jaqui knew it was true. Had she not brought the cartel into their lives her cousin would not have been taken. She stood up, releasing Mo and turning her back. She would get Nettie back.

"Don't do that," Tay's growled order had her stopping in her tracks. "Don't allow her or anyone to blame you. What the hell have I told you a dozen times? It's not your fault some asshole has targeted you. It sure as fuck ain't your fault he came and took Nettie. Now, you." He pointed to Mo. "Shut the fuck up. I'm assuming since you just woke up, you have nothing helpful to say so keep your damn mouth shut."

Jaqui wanted to kiss the man. He was right and she needed to quit blaming herself for the actions of others.

"I'm sorry Nettie was taken, Mo. But it's not my fault. We'll do what we can to get her back, but if you ever hit me again, I'll beat the living shit out of you. Consider that your one free pass." She turned and strolled to the closet, watching as Kai systematically destroyed what was once a wooden panel, exposing the hidden door.

"Motherfucker," Kai swore as he opened the door and they all watched as lights illuminated stairs going down. "Let's go. Sully, stay with the cousin until the paramedics get here. Make sure she gets to the hospital safely as well," he corrected as Jaqui gave him an imploring look. She may be pissed as hell at her cousin, but she didn't want anything to happen to her.

# Chapter Twelve

Tay wanted to wrap his arms around Jaqui and promise all would be okay. Hell, he wanted to take her back to her parents' house and leave her there while they handled the situation, but knew he'd have a fight on his hands. Instead, he made sure she was in the middle as they went down the steps into the unknown. Stealth and speed, had them all moving quickly.

Again, Kai held up a fist, signaling they stop. Voices carried up to them. He recognized the deep baritone of Reece and felt his muscles bunch. He noticed Jaqui readying to jump ahead, and placed his hand on her arm. Her shining blue eyes looked at him over her shoulder, and he saw worry for her cousin in their depths.

"I'm not sure who you fellas are, but this is a private area of my employer. Probably just took the wrong turn and one of the staffers left a door unlocked. It's happened before. If you could just follow me, I'll lead you back out to the casinos floor." Reece sounded almost cordial.

Tay met Kai's gaze and gave a jerky nod. The instant deep-seated knowledge that his team was with him leveled his doubts and fears. He hoped Jaqui felt the same.

A rapid fire of Spanish was spoken, then Reece's deep voice explaining he didn't speak Spanish.

"Listen, if you let me go I won't go to the police," Nettie cried out.

"You stupid punta. You're only alive because the boss wants you. Keep talking and I'll shove something in that hole of yours."

Jaqui froze at the threat, and he knew she didn't want her cousin hurt.

"Well now, isn't that nice. You kiss your mama with that mouth, boy. I reckon you think all the girls love you cause you're handsome. Well, let me tell you, you look like you're so high you can sit on Wednesday and see both Sundays." Nettie's voice dripped sugar.

"What the hell does that even mean?" Reece asked.

"I think these asshats are higher than a kite, and they really do have potty mouths don't you think? Ow, fucker." Nettie's words were cut off by the sound of flesh hitting flesh.

"Now, I was willing to let you walk out of here. Of course, I was going to put my foot down on you taking the girl. However, it's now come to my attention that with just the three of you, and myself, I still have pretty good odds." Reece's voice raised.

Tay raised his brows and wondered if the other man knew they were there.

"You think you are a match for the three of us and our guns, hombre?"

Tay knew Kai had stopped waiting when the other man's fist dropped, and the hand on the knob turned. In a calculated move, Kai rolled across the concrete floor of the basement to the casino. Bullets pinged against the door, and then Coyle followed, leaving him and Jaqui inside. Knowing their positions were compromised, he gave her a quick hard kiss. "Don't get hurt, woman."

She opened the door and they both rolled out to the sound of gunshots. Tay felt a bullet graze his arm, but he got up on one knee, aimed and fired in quick succession. It was over within seconds.

Reece had been smart, grabbing Nettie and rolling her body behind a trash bin as soon as the bullets started flying. The three men who'd taken her had turned at the sound of gunfire, and returned it.

"Well, damn. That was easy," Kai groused, strolling over to one of the men crawling away.

Tay kicked the gun away from another man, then made sure he was dead. Coyle stood over another and shook his head. "This one ain't getting up," Coyle said.

"Neither is this one." Tay indicated the one by his feet.

Reece and Nettie came out, and Jaqui walked over to her cousin, waiting for the recriminations like Mo had given her.

"That was so awesome. Wait till I tell Shep I was in a real live gun fight." Nettie held her hand up like she wanted a high five.

"Do you have a fever?" Jaqui asked, holding her hand up to the woman's forehead.

Nettie shook her head then laughed. "Did you see yourself roll out and start shooting? Woop, girl, you are the things we talk about when we sit on the porch and drink iced tea. I mean not you specifically, but what we'd do if we were ever, you know, like accosted. You are my hero, Jaqui Wallace." Nettie hugged Jaqui with such strength that Tay was shocked his woman didn't feel a rib crack.

"Are you okay? Did they hurt you?" Jaqui stepped away, brushing tears from under her eyes.

Nettie shook her head. "No, I voluntarily went with them when they entered the bedroom. I told them if they took Mo, I'd scream the place down and everyone would hear. They looked nervous and agreed. How's Mo?"

Tay stepped up. "Sully was staying with her until she was checked over at the hospital. Hell, this was over before the ambulance may have even gotten here. She woke up before we followed you guys down here."

Relief washed over features very similar to Jaqui's. "I don't think they knew who was who. They kept looking at Mo, then me, and asked which one of us was Jaqui Wallace. I was scared if I said neither, they'd shoot us both so I lied."

"You did good, girlfriend." Jaqui squeezed her cousin once more. "Let's go back up and check on Mo."

Kai nodded. "I've got a cleanup crew coming. This one is still alive, so we might be able to get some information out of him. Did they say where they were taking you? Tay, you need a medic?"

Tay looked at the wound on his arm, then shook his head. "Oz can just bandage me up and give me a shot or some shit for infection."

Kai looked closer at the wound. "Hell, it's barely a scratch."

Nettie shook her head. "Sorry, mostly they were muttering in another language. Spanish I think. The only Spanish words I know are Margarita and a few things like yes, please and the universal word for no."

Reece laughed. "You are surely a handful for your boyfriend."

Her cousin's face flamed. "I do believe he has said that a couple times."

Back up in the suite, Jaqui couldn't meet Mo's eyes, and Tay wanted to throttle the other woman. Luckily, the paramedics came, and agreed she should be seen at the ER.

"I better call our parents." Nettie sounded less enthusiastic.

Reece looked around the destroyed penthouse. "I guess I better call my employer."

"Shit, sorry man," Sully muttered as they all looked around.

"Nah, he's thrown house parties that damaged a lot worse. He'll just be angry he didn't get laid in the process." Reece gave a weary look toward the gurney taking Mo away.

"When will this be over?" Jaqui asked.

"We will get him, sunshine." Tay wanted to soothe all her pain away.

He left the words unsaid of what would happen if they didn't. Meaning her entire family would be a target until they did.

"Commander Lee is setting up a safe house for your family, Jaqui. He has men enroute to the hospital. Let's go."

Jaqui and Tay followed behind with Oz taking up the rear. He felt as though a huge bullseye was drawn on the woman he loved, and he hated it with every fiber of his being.

"Stop it, Tay." She grabbed his hand.

They walked back out of the elevator. With the paramedics leading the way, the casino seemed to understand something was going on, and several patrons stopped playing their machines as they passed.

Out of the corner of his eye he thought he saw a familiar face. One he didn't think would be in the casino and out in the open. He tapped Jaqui's hand three times, letting her know there was danger, then casually strolled ahead of Kai as if he was taking the lead with Jaqui in tow. The action was out of character, which would alert the other man that something was up.

Once they stepped outside he spoke with as much calm as he could so only Kai could hear. "Medellin is inside the casino. We can't do shit or he could kill hundreds of innocents inside. Shit!"

Tay looked up and down the strip.

"Let's get to the hospital, then once we have Jaqui's family secure we'll rendezvous with Lee and go from there." Kai's tone didn't change, yet Tay knew he was bracing for a battle.

"I don't want my mother to know. She has enough to deal with right now." He'd never heard Jaqui be so stern, and it made him want her even more.

With Nettie and Mo riding together in the ambulance, the team all filed into one of the military SUVs, after Kai and Tay both made sure it was secure. He was getting tired of always looking over his shoulder, especially when Jaqui's very life was at stake. Dammit, he wanted to spend a week or ten where the two of them did nothing but bask on the beach and enjoy the sun, and each other, with nothing to worry about but what they were going to do for dinner.

Carefully, Kai drove them back through Vegas traffic, the large vehicle sticking out like a sore thumb amongst the sports cars and cabs. At the entrance there were several military men waiting, their expressions full of anticipation.

Tay climbed out, and let Kai deal with them. He reached back and pulled Jaqui with him, uncaring what others saw or thought. He would make sure everyone knew they had to go through him to get to her.

"You constantly amaze me, Tay." She kissed his cheek.

Her unguarded expression was a balm to his soul. Never had such a simple action given him the content he felt, even in the middle of one of the most stressful times.

"I see Nettie pacing. I'm going to go check on Mo," Jaqui said.

He frowned as he looked over to see the bodyguard Reece standing outside the doors. "Have we done a thorough background search on the bodyguard, Kai?"

Kai's dark gaze took in the scene. "Commander Lee said he was good."

Tay gave a nod, then walked over to where Jaqui stood talking to her cousin. Wariness had her standing stiff, and he knew it was because of the danger they were in.

"I know it's for our protection, but I'd rather go home. Shep has guns. Lots of guns and knows how to use them." Nettie mentioned her boyfriend who clearly was a real southern boy.

"Nettie, do we look like we don't have guns, and know how to use them?" Jaqui stood with her blonde hair falling in a braid down her back with black cargo pants on and a black T-shirt. She definitely looked the part of a badass fighter. The rest of the team sported similar outfits, making them stand out in the middle of the ER with their guns and military stances.

Nettie chewed her lip. "Mo is sorry for what she said, Jaq. You should go in and see her."

"I don't have time. Listen, just do whatever you're told and make sure your sister does the same. I'll text you to get an update." Jaqui held her hand up as Nettie opened her mouth. "Seriously, Annette, I don't have the time to deal with this right now. See those men." She nodded to the men in full camo. "They are your personal guards who will transport you and Mo to a safe house. Do exactly what they tell you. Don't fuck around with either of you two's safety."

Tay could see Nettie wanted to argue, and was done with watching Jaqui hold back the tears. "We need to go. Reece, how did you know there were intruders in the back entrance?"

"I have alarms set up. When it went off, I made my way back toward the hidden entrance and waited. It didn't take a genius to realize they were carting off an unwilling woman," Reece grunted.

Kai stepped forward. "How were you planning to take on three armed men?"

The grin Reece gave them would have made a lesser man shiver. "Your background check was only surface, boys. You might want to have a little deeper look, Taylor Rouland, or have your girl do it. I'm pretty sure one of you will find out more than the others."

With that Reece walked away.

"Well shit. I hate puzzles." Tay stared after the retreating form of the big guy.

"I believe he's trying to tell us he's on our side, and we just don't know where he fits in. Maybe he's with an alphabet, and we missed that connection." Kai had his hands on his hips, his frown made others give them a wide berth.

"That's just fucking great. So, we have one or more of the alphabet already in place, plus more coming in. How do we know who's friendly and who's not?" Tay arched a brow.

****

Jaqui was wondering the same damn thing. However, knowing the man who had been guarding Mo's supposed boyfriend was actually working for the government, made her feel better about leaving her cousins. Although, she still wanted to slap Mo silly, she also understood why her cousin had slapped her. Not that she was ready to make nice and pretend it didn't happen.

"I'm going to visit with my mom and dad. I'll meet you back at the entrance in an hour." Jaqui turned away before either Tay or Kai could say a word.

Knowing the hospital was virtually crawling with military personnel she still didn't let her guard down until reaching her mom's room. The officer outside the door verified her name, satisfying a deep seeded need for her parents' security.

Not knowing what to expect, she was pleasantly surprised to find her mom sitting up, looking much healthier than the last time she'd seen her. "Mom, you look so much better. How're you feeling?" She rushed to her side, stopping before she kissed the pale cheek.

"Much better. Come here, you." Laci Wallace held out her arm that wasn't broken.

Trying not to hurt her mother, Jaqui leaned down and hugged her. "When do you get to blow this popcorn stand?"

"Don't try to distract me with words. Explain." Her mom pointed at Jaqui's attire.

Shit! Lying wouldn't work. "We had a situation." That much was true. "Don't ask any more, mom. You know I would tell you if I could."

The door opened, and Jaqui felt all the blood drain from her face.

"I wouldn't try anything stupid, chica, unless of course you wish to see your family die in front of you." Jose Medellin moved aside as two other men came in with automatic weapons trained on her aunt and mother.

"What do you want?" She gasped when one of the men came up to her mother's bed.

"You will come with me without a fight, without alerting anyone, and nobody will be hurt. I will leave my man here until we are clear. Once I give him the signal, he will leave without anyone being the wiser. If I do not make that call, he will put a bullet in each of their heads." His bald statement was said with such a lack of inflection, it was as if he was reciting the weather.

She swallowed down the bile threatening to come up. "I'll do whatever you ask. Just leave my family alone."

"Ah, I knew you were a smart one. Let's go before your lover and his friends come looking." His free hand raised, palm up expecting her to take it. Even though her skin was crawling she took it. The gun at her back was immediately taken and shoved into the back of Jose's dress slacks. "You won't be needing that."

"If either of these two make a move to alert the authorities, kill them," Jose ordered before pulling her toward the door.

Jose's unyielding and stoic features held no warmth, and she knew he meant every word. "Do as he says mom, Aunt Laci. Everything will be fine." The lie tripped off her tongue.

Laci nodded. Her mother looked horrified, which only made Jaqui want to rip Jose's balls off and shove them down his throat one by one. She kept her own features placid, knowing they needed to move out before Tay came looking for her.

"We need to move out before my boyfriend comes looking," she said.

Jose laughed. "Oh, I think I have them a little distracted."

His words made her heart clench, but he pulled her out the door. She risked a glance back toward her mom's bed noticing the cell phone under the hand with the cast. The slight light she saw had her breath catching in her throat.

"Let's go," Jose ordered.

She barely kept from stumbling as she got a glimpse at the young man who was outside the door. No longer was it the one who'd marked her off, but a new one who was clearly on the cartel's payroll. The glassy eyed look unmistakable.

"Do you not want to know where I am taking you?" Jose asked breaking into her morose thought.

Pretending a nonchalance she didn't feel, Jaqui kept quiet.

"Ah, such a pity. I thought you'd be a more spirited one. I bet I will get you to...loosen up though." He stared at her with unblinking black eyes.

She narrowed her eyes at him. "Good luck, Jose."

His shocked expression almost made her smile. The hand holding her upper arm bit into the flesh to the point she wanted to cry out. They passed a man in scrubs, his worried expression had her giving him a slight shake of her head. He looked away and pretended to speak into his cell about a patient he'd just seen.

Jose was smiling widely by the time they stepped out of the hospital. A few feet from the curb sat a silver Mercedes with blacked out windows. "Not much further, and then your friends and family will never see you again. I bet you wish you'd have done things differently, hmm?"

She scowled at him. "Like what? Die in Columbia? Or how about gutted you instead of allowing you to have hit a defenseless woman. Oh, you're such a big man aren't you Medellin. I am sure the only way you can truly get it up is if you have a woman or man, subdued. Hell, maybe not even then," she sneered. "Let's not even talk about the fact you're such a fucking pussy you can't take a woman on without her either being drugged or tied up. Yeah, you are such a big man." The last word she spat.

Her words did exactly what she'd wanted, making the man come to a stop, his body vibrating with anger. "You think to question my masculinity." He beat his fist against his chest. "I squash men three times your size. I have women falling at my feet to be with me. I want nothing more than to show the world I do not allow prisoners to escape. You will be an example of what happens to those who do." His breathing was harsh, spittle flew from his mouth with each word, and his voice had risen so loud they'd drawn a small crowd.

Jaqui knew her window of opportunity would be small, and the fact the doctor would have alerted security as they'd been coming from her mother's room. She was gambling a lot, but knowing if she got in the car with Jose and his men, she'd never see anyone she loved again. Hell, she feared he'd splatter her brains all over the leather seats without blinking an eye.

Standing in the hot Vegas sun, she watched him lift his arm. Time stood still. At this close a range there was no way he'd miss. A red dot appeared on his forehead, making her smile.

"You might want to freeze, Jose," she smirked.

"Why would I do that?" His arm with the gun pointed at her chest.

"I see a nice red dot on your forehead. You can shoot me, but you'll die as well." She shrugged while her heart threatened to burst out of her chest.

"Well, I guess I'll take you with me," he said then pulled the trigger.

A heavy weight landed on her at the same moment, knocking her to the ground. She expected pain, or darkness. When she opened her eyes she saw Tay lying on top of her while her ears rang.

"Answer me damn it," Tay yelled in a harsh voice.

"I'm fine. I think." She spoke around the lump in her throat, then buried her face in his neck. She could feel his heart beating erratically against her palm.

"Jaqui Wallace, I swear to all that is holy you are going to be the death of me. You are the joy in my world. My life was lifeless before you. If I never see you with a gun pointed at you for the rest of my life, it will be too soon." His bent and covered her mouth with his.

She curled her arms around him, pulling him closer until he was almost flush with her on the hard pavement.

"You two might want to cut that shit out, you're gathering a crowd. This might be Vegas and all, but

I'm pretty sure what you two want to do is highly illegal even here." Kai's amused voice made her gasp against Tay's lips.

"Love you too, Kai." Tay pushed up, then held his hand out for Jaqui.

A white sheet covered a body. "Oh, shit. Is he dead?" She looked between Kai and Tay.

"It was either him or you." Kai didn't look remorseful at all.

Jaqui eyed the body of the man who'd threatened her family. "Shit, he left a man with my mom and aunt."

Kai patted her shoulder. "No worries. We've taken him into custody as well."

"I need to see them." She shook off imaginary dust, feeling a few aches from her fall to the ground.

"I'll go with you. Do you need me here?" Tay questioned Kai.

"Go ahead. We've got this under control." Kai and several teams had amassed to keep onlookers from the scene.

In the second Jose had fired, Kai had shot him dead. Jaqui felt nothing for the man or his death. Luckily for them he'd had a silencer on his gun as did Kai. The entire scene played out with civilians none the wiser. "Could you imagine being so naïve?" She asked as Tay escorted her back through the corridors.

"I think it could be great. Imagine walking around without a care in the world." Tay sounded amused.

## Chapter Thirteen

After checking on her parents, the last thing she wanted to do was go back to their home or a casino. She wanted to spend a little quiet time where she and Tay had never been, with just the two of them, however Kai and the rest of the team wanted to celebrate.

Now, sitting at the bar with a bunch of drunk SEALs, she found herself laughing at their antics. Tay sat straddling a chair, his arms draped over the back as he watched her with heat as she took another shot. A full body shiver shook her. "What the hell was that one?" She licked her bottom lip, enjoying the tart flavor left behind.

"That was what is affectionately called a Purple Hooter." Kai tapped his finger on the table.

Oz signaled the waitress over. "We need six Scooby Snacks."

Jaqui smiled. "Dude, I am not eating a freaking dog biscuit."

"Oh, girl. This drink is so good you'll want to have like ten of them." Oz folded his arms over his massive chest.

She eyed the men sitting around the table. "What is in that?" She looked at the green concoction and then the guys.

"Coconut Rum, Crème de Bananas, Melon Liqueur, Pineapple Juice and Half & Half." Coyle licked his lips.

"That sounds like Kool-Aid for kids. Jaqui likey." She grabbed the larger than average shot glass.

A male groan sounded beside her, but she ignored it as she gulped the delicious liquor.

"Holy shit, that is delicious. Can I get a glass of that?" She licked her lips.

"Okay, enough. It's time to go." Tay stood and waved at the guys. "Come on, half pint." Tay lifted her out of the seat.

"But, Tay, I was having fun." Jaqui giggled. "You know, like from that scene from one of those eighties movies where the guy carried his woman out of the factory.

"Sweetheart, that was Richard Gere, and he was not a Navy SEAL." Tay flagged down a cab outside the club without letting her down.

"You can put me down." She snuggled closer.

He rubbed his head over the top of hers. "Not yet."

In truth, she was starting to feel the effects of the alcohol. "Did I use my outside voice again?"

Tay winced. "Your outside voice is quite loud, sunshine." He instructed the driver which hotel they were staying at.

He pulled Jaqui closer and began a soothing rub over her arms. "You and I need to have a talk when you're sober."

She rested her head on his chest, enjoying his warmth and simple touch, yet his words alarmed her. "Yeah, we do."

Tay froze mid-stroke. "That sounds scary."

"You, the big bad SEAL who can face off against terrorists, but is scared of one wee little female," she scoffed.

He looked down, and a hundred words were conveyed in his eyes. "Before you I had my team, but now with you, I have so much more to lose."

The cab came to a stop and Tay gave him more than enough to cover the trip.

"Come on. We'll talk more upstairs." Tay let her slide out and after making sure she could walk, he kept a protective arm around her waist.

"You really are the sweetest man."

Inside the elevator, she leaned heavily against the back wall. Being surrounded by four sides of mirrors, she looked at her and Tay standing side-by-side. "We really do look good together," she murmured. "Our baby would've been adorable," she said on a sad sigh.

Tay's head whipped around. "What do you mean?"

How she wished she could blame her loose tongue on alcohol. "I'll explain in the room. I'm going to need to sit down."

She was saved by the doors opening on their floor, then had no choice as Tay grabbed her hand and pulled her along with him. The trepidation she thought she'd feel was absent.

"Alright, explain." Tay rounded on her when they entered.

She kicked her shoes off, then sat on the king bed. Without looking at him, she explained about the pregnancy and then the miscarriage. She always hated silence. Silence to her meant thinking. Which usually ended with someone coming to conclusions that were not good.

"Why didn't you tell me?" His ragged voice made her look up.

She snorted. "Really?"

****

Tay shook his head. He understood why she hadn't told him. Hell! He thought back to the second time he'd made love to her that afternoon. "I wore a condom but didn't check to see if it broke. I mean I don't think it did completely, and then the text came through. I was such a dick. I'm shocked you even talked to me." His eyes blazed with passion and regret.

"Well, I have had a while to forgive you. Do you forgive me for not telling you?"

He scooped her up and sat back with her in his lap. "There is nothing to forgive you for. We can't replace what we lost, but we can always try for another when the time is right."

From the look in her eyes, he thought she might agree to his next words. "Jaqui, when I first met you I was…how do I put it? A man with a mission, but not fulfilled. I swear I had all these jagged parts of me until you. You smooth those edges out and make me a better man."

"My mom said I was always a lost girl with my head up in the clouds. I don't know how accurate that was, but since joining the Navy I didn't feel so lost. When I met you my feet didn't seem to touch the ground when I was with you. I thought, this is the guy I want to be with forever. If I had to be lost, he was the one I wanted to get lost with. If I could chase stars, you would be the one I'd want to do it with."

His smile felt like it was going to split his cheeks. "Do you know that is the exact way I'd express how I felt about you. You made me feel like a man, yet made me want to be a boy. Sort of like a grown up version of Peter Pan. Only with guns and shit." Her burst of laughter had him bending to stifle it with his lips.

"I couldn't stop thinking of you. Even now I can't think of you being in danger. I know," he stopped her words with a quick kiss. "I'm not asking you to give up your career in the Navy. I'll have to come to grips with it, it's just hard to think about the woman you love with all your heart in danger."

"I've been thinking about that, too. My reenlistment is coming up. I was thinking of not, but I want to be near you. I mean I don't want to be clingy or…" She looked away.

Tay used his hand to turn her back to face him. "Presume away. I want you with me every day and night that we can be. When I'm not on a mission that is."

"I love Hawaii. I could find a little bungalow near base and I'm sure I could find a job."

He stopped her flow of words with a thumb to her lips. "Jaqui, there is something I want to ask you. I had it all prepared, but this sort of pushed it forward and isn't where I wanted to do it, but it feels right." He lifted her up, then placed her on the edge of the bed, getting down on one knee. "You deserve a grand proposal, and I am not worthy, but if you give me the chance I will be the best husband you could ever ask for. I'll be there with you when you want to reach the stars, and do everything in my power to help you achieve your goals. I'll gladly float up in the clouds with you, and when our kids have kids, I want to be sitting next to you on the beach watching them make sandcastles. And when we're old and grey, I'll still love you to the moon and back and be there telling you how much I love you. You are the smooth to my jagged edges. If you say no, I'll keep asking until you say yes, because you are worth it. I may not be worthy, but dammit you are."

She hiccupped then launched herself into his arms. "That was the sweetest, most romantic thing I've ever heard. Screw Richard Gere, he is so not worthy. God, I love you Taylor Rouland. Oh my gawd. I'm going to be Jaqui Rouland." She peppered kisses all over his face.

"We will get a ring tomorrow." He promised.

"Do you want a big wedding?" Jaqui asked.

He tilted his head to the side. "I'm good with whatever you want, whenever you want it."

"How about we have a pre-wedding honeymoon tonight, then get married tomorrow." His dick jerked beneath his jeans as the woman of his dreams stood up and lifted her shirt over her head. The plain white cotton bra was sexier because of the stark contrast to her tan skin. With her legs straddling him, she unsnapped the button on her cargo pants. The hiss of her zipper going down echoed in the room.

"You just gonna sit there, or get nekkid." Uncertainty filled her cornflower blue eyes.

He reached up and pulled her down. "Are you serious? You'll marry me tomorrow? What about your parents?" Tay didn't want to get ahead of himself, but if she was truly on board with getting hitched in Vegas, he would have her before the justice of the peace or at a little white chapel before she could change her mind.

"We can do a big party after they are both out of the hospital, but I don't need or want a huge wedding. We can invite them to Hawaii and do a big luau, and invite both families and our friends."

With her sitting astride him with her pants undone in the white bra, she looked too sweet for words. He licked his lips, then closed the space between them, nibbling on her neck until he had her moaning. She wrapped both arms around his neck, and he slipped his tongue into her mouth, claiming her with a thoroughness that would have frightened him, had he not just asked her to marry him.

He stroked one hand down her back and cupped her ass, pulling her closer. "God you smell good." Their tongues dueled as they continued to kiss, becoming more restless, needing more than just a kiss.

It was Jaqui who pulled away breathless. She closed her eyes and rested against his forehead, sucking in air. The urge to strip every stitch of clothing from her body and pound into her was almost overwhelming. His cock ached for her.

"Up, Jaqui. I want to make love to you on that bed, not the floor like some randy teenager."

She snorted, and he gave her a mock scowl, then tickled her side, making her breasts bounce.

Jaqui stood and held her hand out. This time it was he who took her hand. He didn't miss the fact they were each willing to help the other. She was his equal.

He reached behind and unsnapped her bra, releasing her breasts. "You're fucking gorgeous." His hands went to work on her pants, taking the panties with them. They hadn't turned the light on, but the room was bathed in light from the strip. "You truly are a goddess come to life. My very own Venus." He stepped back and reached behind him, pulling his own T-shirt off. He stripped his jeans and kicked his shoes off, leaving him as naked as she.

"I think you're the amazing one." He started to deny her, but she stopped him. "No, don't. You are. I mean look at you. Every inch of you is sculpted to perfection. Not to mention this guy seems to always be up and ready to go." Her soft hand gripped his shaft.

The awe in her voice made him want to be all that and more, and he wanted to wrap her in bubble wrap to keep her safe forever.

"What's put that look on your face?" She asked, stroking him.

He sighed. "I want to put you in a bubble and keep you safe."

"You can't, but you can love me."

Ignoring the frantic beating of his heart, he placed his hand over hers, stopping the stroking. "Oh, I love you alright. We will definitely have time, but not if you keep doing that." He kissed her temple then her cheek, following down to her jaw, then the corners of her mouth. "All the time in the world, sunshine," he promised.

"Tay." His name was little more than a whisper.

"I want you more than I want my next breath," he told her. Slowly he ran his hands down her shoulders until they covered both her perfect breasts. "I'm not the kind of man for flowery words, but with you I swear I have never wanted a woman the way I want you."

Her breasts were soft in his rough hands, and he bent to brush his mouth over the tips. She gave a breathy gasp and grabbed the back of his head. He took that as a good sign and continued to tease the tip with his tongue, working the other with his thumb over the distended tip. Jaqui gasped and then moaned making him even harder.

He had to swallow against the moan he felt vibrating out of his own body. Every cell cried out for him to toss her on the bed and claim her. With his dick throbbing, he was close to coming, but he ignored his own needs and focused on pleasuring his wife to be.

The smooth skin of her body under his hands, the bold thrust of her hips begging for more, the tender grip of her fingers in his hair, all designed to torture him.

It took monumental effort to lift his head from her, when all he truly wanted to do was continue. Instead he lifted her onto the bed.

She licked her lips and he groaned at the thought of her lips surrounding his cock. "Don't do that."

"What?" She blinked innocently up at him.

He shook his head. "You are sensual without even trying." Straddling her legs, every muscle in Jaqui's body tensed. Her nipples tightened and a bolt of masculine pride went through him. His cock bobbed against his stomach, but he ignored it and leaned down to pleasure her. Leaning forward he licked first one nipple, then the next, blowing a cool breath of air over the wet tips.

She moaned his name when he plumped the firm mounds in his palms. He placed a sucking kiss on each tip, then moved down her body, pressing open mouthed kisses on each rib, remembering the bruises she'd had which now were only slightly discolored. He reached her mound, moved so his legs were in between hers, spreading her open. "Damn, baby. You're wet."

"What the hell did you think I'd be?" Her legs moved restlessly.

He ran his thumbs between her slit, exposing the tiny pearl at the top. "Exactly what I see. My woman hot, wet, and ready for me." With those words, Tay leaned forward and swirled his tongue around her clit, treating her like the favorite treat she was. He hummed, making her moan and pant, her chest rose and fell.

He continued to lick and tease, burying his face between her thighs. Tay worked her with his lips and tongue and teeth, loving the sounds she made. His tongue probed her opening, then worked back up to her clit. He felt her hand grabbing the back of his head, her whimpers escalating and he chuckled.

"Tay, I'm going to come so hard the neighbors are gonna hear," she swore.

Using his tongue, he curled it over the hard bundle of nerves at the apex of her thighs, wanting to test her theory. He flicked the little bundle, and lapped at it until she thrashed beneath him. When he inserted one, then two fingers inside her, she went wild, arching up. Her legs clamped around his head, they shook and her scream was muffled by a pillow she'd pulled over her face. He continued to move his fingers in and out, letting her ride out the orgasm before he removed them. Using his free hand he tossed the pillow off, then met her eyes while he licked his fingers.

"That was off the charts amazing," she gasped.

"Oh, that was just the beginning, but you cheated." He nodded toward the pillow.

She pouted up at him. "I was just preserving your ears."

Tay scooted up so they were face to face, bracing his weight on his forearms. "When we are home, you will scream for me and nobody will be near."

Nodding, Jaqui lifted her hips, her pussy rubbed against his hard cock, making them both shudder.

"Let me get a condom."

When he went to get up, she stopped him. "I'm on the shot. I mean after…well, after what happened before, I didn't want anything like that happening again. Not until I was ready and until I was with the man I loved. I haven't been with anyone but you." She looked away.

He used the hands next to her head to hold her so she was facing me. "You know you were the last woman I've been with, and will be the last until my dying day."

Her eyes widened, a tear leaked out. "I love you so much."

"To the moon and back, I love you." Tay kissed away her tears, then ran the head of his cock through her folds. He coated his erection with her juices, stroking her clit with each pass, making Jaqui moan and brought him close to coming before he ever entered her.

Shifting his legs, he maneuvered them so he was between both of hers, then reached down and found her entrance and pushed inside. They'd made love before, but this time the experience seemed more profound. Her small body clung to him and he grabbed both of her hands in each of his, entwining their fingers as he began a slow and steady pace.

He pulled almost all the way out, then glided back in with a smooth thrust. Over and over again, he continued. Their eyes locked, he felt her legs lift and wrap around his waist, making it harder for him to pull so far back.

Tay angled his hips and hit her clit with each thrust, making sure to grind their pelvis together with each stroke. She bucked against him, panting.

"Yes, just like that, Tay. Faster, please."

He lost control of his thrust at her plea and began to move faster and harder. The feel of her body getting closer and closer to orgasm made him more aware of his own impending release. He slid out and then in, increasing his speed until he no longer had any control, completely lost in the need to find pleasure. The tight rippling around his cock snapped the last of his control, and he growled like an animal and fucked her harder. His head lowered and he kissed her hard. The savage kiss would probably bruise her lips. She cried out and then he felt her pussy spasm around him, and then hard jets of semen filled her. He'd tried to stop and let her ride out her own before he found his, but the sensation was too great.

After he was sure he had nothing left to give, he buried his face in her neck and breathed deeply, then rolled taking her with him. Even now, he could feel tiny ripples along his dick from her orgasm, and continued to rock into her.

****

Jaqui shivered and held onto Tay like a lifeline in a storm. A completely contented grin crossed her face. "Damn, that was off the charts awesome." She kissed his chin.

"I'm glad you think so. I think you broke me." He nuzzled the top of her head.

"How did I break you?" She asked, hating when he slipped out of her.

He canted his head to the side. "My dick. I think you broke it."

Laughing she tried to pinch his side. "No fair. You have no fat to pinch."

Tay grinned. "I'll take that as a compliment."

Yawning they both settled down into the bed until Jaqui felt goosebumps from the air-conditioning.

"You cold?" He didn't wait for her to respond, instead hopped up and went into the bathroom. A minute later he returned with a warm wash cloth. Jaqui squealed as he put it between her thighs. "Tay, I can do that."

"Yep, so can I." He held her down easily. When he was finished, he tossed the rag toward the open bathroom door, then walked over to the big windows and shut the curtains, making the room go dark. He didn't seem to have a problem navigating the room, and then the bed dipped as he maneuvered her under the blankets, then climbed in beside her."

"Get some rest, sunshine. When the sun rises I'm taking you to the first chapel you agree to after we buy rings. I'm sure we can get Kai and Nettie to stand up for us." He ran his hand up her smooth back.

She thought about it and nodded. "Sounds good. Should I text her now. You never know about her, she could hop the first flight back to Shep. There's something about that man, but I promised not to check into him. You however, did not make that promise."

Tay groaned. "I can see how your mind is working, and I like it."

"I'll show you how much I appreciate your cooperation as soon as I get some sleep." She yawned so hard her jaw hurt.

"Get some sleep, baby. I'll hold you to your promise later."

Jaqui woke up before Tay and felt like she had someone banging around in her skull. She crawled out of bed, trying not to wake him.

"Where you going?"

"Why are you being so loud? Loud is rude. Loud when someone has had too much to drink the night before is a killing offense. However, you were sober right?" She squinted at his delicious looking body barely covered by the sheet.

He nodded, but didn't answer.

"Good, so then you can't take back the proposal. I'm going to shower, while you go procure something for this thing kicking my head. Then, we are going on our first mission." She went back over and gave him a kiss on his cheek. "Morning breath, so no kiss on the mouth for you."

She shuffled into the bathroom and heard him laugh. "Love you too," she called from inside the too bright room. "Why the fuck do they make these rooms so damn neon for crying out loud."

The door opened, and a naked Tay came in. "Come on, let's conserve water and I'll help you wash your hair. It'll make you feel better." He held two tablets in his palm. "I also had these in my pocket. I'm a former boy scout."

"Oh, bless you." She grabbed a glass from next to the sink and rinsed it out then filled it with water.

"Is it bad?" He rubbed her shoulders, then massaged her neck.

"Not like I want to stab my eyes out. No. I have had worse."

Tay reached in and turned the water on. By the time they showered, and he was true to his word, and helped her wash and condition her hair, she felt much better.

"We will have shower sex next time," she swore.

He nearly fell off the bed at her announcement. "Do you just spout this shit out to make me hard?"

Jaqui finished doing a side braid. "Uh, why would you think that? I was just thinking it was a lost opportunity, and really wanted to experience that with you."

He stood up and wrapped his arms around her. "I am the luckiest son-of-a-bitch."

Jaqui patted his back. "Remember that when I mess up, or don't cook very well."

# Chapter Fourteen

"What do you mean you are getting married? You can't. I mean...don't you want the big church and all that hoopla shit?" Nettie asked.

"Nope, I just want to marry Tay. Once everyone is out of the hospital and cleared for travel we'll do a big party in Hawaii."

A stunned silence met her announcement.

"What about Mo? You know she feels awful for hitting you. I think you should ask her to come too. She's been released from the hospital and is a hot mess thinking you hate her," Nettie's voice became a whisper.

Jaqui looked over at Tay as he held his cell to his ear. "I don't hate her, I thought she hated me."

"Good gawd, sugar. I will take a switch to both your hides. Alright, you tell me when and where and Mo and I'll be there. Please tell me you aren't wearing camo. I mean I'm all for country-chic, but I draw the line at that. You best find a nice dress, or I'll bring you something slutty and Mo and I will hold you down and dress you."

"I plan to go in ten minutes. We are going ring shopping and then getting proper attire at the shops in Caesars." She pulled the phone away at the loud screech.

"Ten minutes? Girl, who's helping you? Seriously, I've seen how you dress. How about Mo and I meet you there in say like thirty, that way you and Tay can pick out a ring, and then we'll help you pick out a dress while he gets a nice suit or something?" Her cousin's tone was serious.

*Damn, do they think I look that bad?* She mouthed to Tay. He shook his head and pulled her onto his lap.

"I'll text you when we finish shopping for a ring." Jaqui disconnected, hearing the words Cartier and Tiffany's being shouted before she hit the end button.

"Sorry about that. Don't think for a minute I expect a huge diamond. Matching bands are fine with me." She looked Tay in the eyes.

327

He grinned. "Sunshine, I already knew that. Now, up with you or I'll have us both nekkid and then your cousins will be banging on the door, while I'm banging you."

Jaqui stood and looked at her outfit. Maybe Nettie had it right. She definitely didn't want to get married in anything resembling military or boyish. "Come on big guy, let's get to shopping."

A while later they walked through glass doors leading to an exclusive boutique where two identical faces were waiting for her. Her heart began to race as she looked at Mo.

Her cousin broke away from Nettie. "I'm such a bitch. Like a bitch of the first order and don't deserve your forgiveness, but I'm asking anyway. Please, Jaq, forgive me and know that I will never raise my hand to you again. Well, I might, but only because I'm an idiot and know you can kick my ass six ways to Sunday."

Jaqui wrinkled up her nose. "I'm pretty sure I can kick your ass in more ways than that, but I already forgave you." Mo wrapped her arms around Jaqui. All the stress and worry evaporated.

"I'm going to leave you ladies here and meet up with the guys to get something decent to wear." Tay looked scared to step into the pricey shop.

She leaned up and kissed the tip of his chin, which he quickly bent and picked her up, covering her mouth with his. She blushed and he laughed when they pulled away. "Go away before you make me jump your bones inside Valentino. I'm sure they've seen lots of scandalous things, but I refuse to add to that list. Besides, I want to find the perfect dress since this is the one and only time I'll ever be getting married."

Tay bent and brushed the tip of his nose against hers, then ran it across her cheek to her neck. At her ear, he stopped. "You'll look gorgeous in anything, but I prefer you in nothing," he whispered stepping back and cupping her face in his big palms. "I promise to be waiting, and I'll even try to keep my hands to myself until the minister pronounces us husband and wife." He kissed her one last time.

"You realize you make me melt right? Like I'm a total puddle of goo right now. How am I supposed to shop, let alone make coherent choices?"

"Baby, you made me a puddle of goo the first time I saw you. The best choice, the only smart thing I've ever done was ask you to be mine forever. When you get tired, I'll be there to carry you. If you're hurt, I'll do everything in my power to fix you and make damn sure whoever was responsible for hurting you pays dearly. You and I are like a puzzle. People may not think we match because I'm all jagged and rough around the edges, but put us together, and we match, making the most beautiful picture. Without you, I'm a jumbled mess is what I'm saying. You make me a better man, and I'll do my best to deserve you for the rest of my life."

A chorus of awe's were echoed behind her. "See? You did it again," she sniffed.

Tay wiped away her tears with his thumbs, smiling down at her. She realized it was moments like these that made all the bad worth it. Her heart and soul belonged to one Navy SEAL. Each moment with him she'd cherish, but the ones where he laid his heart out for her and all to see were precious.

"Now you know how you make me feel each time you smile. Now, go see if you can find anything as beautiful as you. I'll see you in a few hours." He gave her one more kiss, then turned and left.

Mo and Nettie watched him leave.

"Hey, quit ogling my man's ass." Jaqui smiled as her cousins pretended to wipe drool off their chins.

"Not our fault your man has a damn fine bum," Nettie said.

Mo nodded. "Let's do this. We ain't got all day."

Nettie chucked at her obvious discomfort. She flipped them both the bird.

Two hours later she had a dress, shoes and the most delicate lingerie she'd ever owned. Her hair and nails were done, and her nerves were frazzled. "Are you sure I look okay?" She asked for the tenth or twentieth time.

"Honestly, you are gorgeous. Tay will probably have a hard time keeping his hands to himself while

331

you say your vows." Mo carried the bag with her dress in it.

All three of them had new dresses and had their hair done. As they entered the Little White Chapel, Jaqui swore butterflies churned in her stomach. They quickly dressed, then Nettie volunteered to check on the men.

"Oh my God. Wait till you see your man. Holy shit! His friends, too." She fanned her face. "I want a SEAL."

Jaqui gulped, wondering what the guys had gotten up to. She knew they couldn't be dressed in their Navy uniforms. "I'm ready."

Mo waved her forward. "Yeah you are. Our parents are going to be pissed, but I'm blaming you and Nettie."

Nettie elbowed Mo. "What's new there."

Jaqui stood outside the closed door to the chapel with her two best friends and cousins in front of her. As the doors opened the wedding march began. Her eyes took in the scene, and she completely forgot all about her nerves as she got her first glimpse of Tay,

Oz, Coyle, Kai and Sully. Holy crap! All five of the guys were dressed in white pants, with white button down shirts and jackets and white shoes. Tay had an orchid pinned to the lapel of his jacket, the only thing that made him stand out, other than he was the most handsome man in her opinion. What stunned her most was seeing the twins friend Traci sitting in the front.

"Oh, forgot to tell you Traci was coming. When she'd heard about Nettie being kidnapped, and me being drugged last night, she insisted on coming to make sure we were okay." Mo smiled over her shoulder.

Jaqui patted her on the arm with her free hand, seeing the gorgeous ring she and Tay picked out glint under the lights. "No problem. I don't mind at all. You can introduce me after. Now move it ladies. I have a man to marry."

Nettie and Mo began the slowest march known to mankind, making Jaqui want to rip their strawberry blonde hair out. By the time she reached the spot next to Tay, the butterflies had calmed. His eyes on her the entire time gave her the resolve she needed, and seeing the absolute love shining back at her, she knew this was a forever kind of thing.

The minister cleared his throat, and then they were repeating after him. When they were announced as husband and wife, she felt complete, as if she had everything she could ever want in the world. She knew without a doubt, no matter what, Tay would be there for her, or make sure someone was when he was unable.

"I will love you for all the days and nights for the rest of my life, Jaqui Rouland." Tay bent and kissed her.

She melted into his embrace, conveying without words her love for him. They were both breathing hard as they pulled away. "I'm going to hold you to that, Taylor Rouland." She covered her mouth with one hand. "I'm Mrs. Rouland. I love you so fucking much."

Kai and the rest of the team laughed.

Oz clapped Tay on the back. "Thank god one of you still cusses like a sailor."

Tay raised his middle finger, making the minister shake his head.

"So, we ready to blow this place and get some grub? I'm starving." Coyle rubbed his belly.

Jaqui noticed Sully watching Traci and her cousins chatting by the front pew. She leaned close to him. "You got a thing for one of my cousins, Sully?"

The gorgeous man blushed. "Um, no, but I do have some disturbing news for your cousin Mo about her boyfriend Alan. Wasn't sure if this was the right time to break it to her." He looked at Kai.

Kai shook his head then stopped. She remembered the only time the team ever held off on saying anything was when they wanted to keep from upsetting the women in their lives. She was torn. She knew keeping secrets could hurt. But knowledge was power, and Mo wasn't alone. "Tell me, and then I'll tell her."

Sully licked his full lips. "Alan Mancini is gay. I don't mean bisexual. I mean straight up, he likes men only."

335

"Damn! Do you think he's been trying to swim in the lady pool, or is he using my cousin as a beard?"

All four men shrugged.

Mo and Nettie pulled Traci up to meet them. Once introductions were made, they all decided to head out for a celebratory dinner.

"I'm going to ride with Tay and the guys. Do you ladies want to ride with us?" Jaqui looked at the stretch Hummer parked outside with the driver waiting next to the back door.

"I rented a car at the airport. How about I meet you there?" Traci offered.

"Mo and I'll ride with you. Won't we, Mo?" Nettie nudged her sister who nodded in agreement.

The ride to the restaurant was filled with more hilarity than she'd have thought as Tay and his fellow SEALs joked and laughed. Trepidation filled her at the news she had to break to Mo, but with Tay's arm around her, she leaned into him and let his strength bolster her. She wanted her cousins to have what she did.

****

Mo wondered how long she had to pretend to be happy. Not that she wasn't genuinely happy for her cousin. Jaqui, next to Nettie was her best friend, then came the wild child Traci. She smiled as the crazy bitch cussed out another driver on the road, glad she was in the backseat and could close her eyes.

"Mo, tell this hooker that she can't just cut someone off and then give them the bird like it was their fault," Nettie yelled.

Traci laughed. "Clearly, I just did."

"She obviously proved she could and done did it. Besides we're here." Mo watched in horror as Traci whipped the sporty little car into a spot that was just vacated, even though another car was clearly already waiting for it.

"I am so not getting out. That car is probably waiting to yell at us, or Bertha is already out and gonna give us a beat down." Nettie put her head in her hands.

"Why does she have to be Bertha?" Traci asked with her hand on the door handle.

"You know everyone in prison has names like Big Bertha or something."

Mo looked up at the ceiling, praying for some divine intervention.

"Your sister needs meds, Mo."

"Hey, you're the one who spends more time with her than me." Mo pointed out.

Traci seemed to ponder that for a moment. "True that. However, she did not come from my side of the family."

"Hello, I'm right here." Nettie jerked the door open. "And for your information, beotches, I am the only stable one in the car."

"Newsflash, you are not in the car," Traci hollered back.

Mo rubbed her temples. "Lord save me."

"Sugar, there ain't no saving you. She's your sister."

"I will so throat punch you, Traci Jones." Mo didn't wait to hear another snarky comment, figuring her sister might already need backup.

Luckily, the vehicle with Jaqui and the others pulled up, making the angry guy drive off without incident. Nettie put herself between Mo and Traci, and began singing, loudly. Her cheerful attitude contagious.

"You are such a goof," Mo swore, jogging across the parking lot with her arm threaded through one of Nettie's.

"I know you are but what am I?" Nettie laughed.

"You're both goofs, which is why I love you." Jaqui hugged Mo and then Nettie. "Traci, how do you put up with them?"

Traci shrugged. "I own a bar called the Naughty Girls."

When they waited for her to elaborate, Nettie snorted. "Picture Coyote Ugly on steroids. The Naughty Girls is the best place to go and get your drink on, your dance on, and you can get up on the bar and karaoke. It's the bomb."

"Please tell me you don't let these two sing there?" Tay asked.

Mo glared. "Hey, I'll have you know we are fabulous. However, I have only been there a few times since I live here."

Nettie put one hand on her hip, the other she pointed at Tay. "I am a local celebrity there. Shep said he knew the first time he saw me on the bar, I was the girl for him."

A look flashed across Traci's features that had her wanting to ask what was up, but the other woman shook her head.

"Hey, Mo, will you go to the ladies room with me?" Jaqui asked as they entered the restaurant and were told they would be seated in a few minutes.

Sighing, she walked alongside Jaqui. She'd grown up with money. Her dad and Jaqui's were best friends and business partners, but her grandparents were mega rich. They didn't flaunt their money, and most didn't realize it.

Jaqui waited until they made sure the bathroom was empty, then she turned to Mo. Before she could open her mouth, Mo held up her hand. "I think I know what you're going to say."

Her cousin shook her head. "I don't know how to even say this."

"Why don't you just say it and then we'll go from there." Mo took a deep breath.

"Are you in love with Alan Mancini?"

She laughed, unable to stop herself. "I figured that's what this was about. Damn nosey men." She paced away from Jaqui. "Alan and I have been friends for years. I'm assuming someone told you about his sexual preference?" At Jaqui's nod, she continued. "He's Italian, and therefore his parents expect him to be a certain way. Since I don't need his money, and I am not in love with anyone right now, it worked for us to let everyone think we were together."

Jaqui blew out a breath. "Thank fuck."

Mo hugged her. "You really do have the mouth of a sailor."

Together they walked back out to find their group waiting. She noticed the one named Sully

341

staring at Traci, but typically her sister's best friend was oblivious.

"I'm starved," Jaqui said, cuddling into Tay's side.

"Everything okay with you?" His eyes went from Jaqui to Mo.

Mo nodded. "Everything is fine, Tay."

## Chapter Fifteen

Tay loved his friends, but he couldn't wait to get his new wife alone. She looked stunning in the strapless white dress that molded to her curves. He was pleased she'd chosen white, knowing he was her first and would be her last lover, she definitely deserved to wear any color she wanted. The glow on her face as she'd walked toward him had his cock hard as stone. It took all his effort not to hurry the minister along, then whisk her away to the closest private area and have his way with her. He could picture himself lifting the gown up to her waist, and taking her from behind, hard and deep, but he'd consoled himself with thoughts of taking his time later.

Later was hours instead of the twenty he'd promised his poor abused dick. She was smiling as he strode down the corridor to the honeymoon suite at Caesars with her in his arms.

"People stared at us." She didn't sound upset.

He didn't care. "They were jealous cause I was carrying the most gorgeous woman in my arms, and she's my wife."

She laughed softly, then moaned when he kissed her. His fingers itched to delve beneath the dress she had on and discover what she had on underneath. "Are you wet?"

"Ssh, people might hear you."

He bit the lobe of her ear. "We're the only ones in the hall, sunshine."

Letting her slide down his body, startled a gasp from her that made him smile. "I bet you are, or will be once I make you come a time or two."

343

She made a small sound of protest as he stepped away to open the door. "Come here." He scooped her back into his arms, carrying her over the threshold.

"You truly are my very own Richard Gere, only better." She trailed the backs of her fingers along his jaw.

"I'm so glad you think so. Now, how about I show you how much I love you."

Inside the huge suite, they bypassed everything and headed straight for the bedroom. "We'll explore the amenities after," he told her.

Jaqui nodded. "I can't wait."

Tay couldn't either. He wanted to undress her and watch her unravel for him. He wanted to feel her pussy surround his cock for the first time as his wife, and watch her face as they both fell apart together.

He found the hidden zipper on the side of the gown, and lowered it. Slowly, he eased it down. Breathing almost became impossible as he found what was beneath. A powder blue strapless corset, and the tiniest pair of matching panties he'd ever seen, graced her tanned body. He nearly swallowed his tongue when he realized she'd had a garter belt on the entire afternoon.

"I do believe you're supposed to take this off." She pointed to the white elastic around her upper thigh.

His mouth watered. Tay tossed his jacket off. The tie and shirt followed, sailing somewhere behind him. Down to the white dress slacks and shoes, he kicked the matching shoes off, then knelt at her feet. "I think I have died and gone to heaven."

Her glazed look let him know she enjoyed looking at him, too. She licked her lips, and he swore he'd have them wrapped around his cock before the night was through. But first, he needed to get her naked.

He smoothed his hands up her legs, starting at her ankles all the way up to her thighs, then he took the same path with his lips. By the time he reached the crease between her thighs, he'd forgotten about the garter. Pulling the bit of fabric down, he helped her step out of it, and added the small thing to the pile. He returned to the vision in front of him, and used his thumbs to spread her pussy open for him to see how wet she was. "You're pretty everywhere." Tay began stroking her from clit to her opening, slow and soft, using his thumbs he pressed them both inside her, making her cry out.

He looked up her body, watching as she shook under his assault, loving her response to his every lick, suck, and nibble. Every intimate kiss brought her closer to orgasm. With her hands holding his head against her, her legs spread apart, she rocked her hips back and forth and rode his face and fingers taking what he gave her.

Finally, when he didn't think he could stand it anymore, he felt the first flutter of sensation around his thumbs. "That's it. Give it to me. Come for me. From now on, all your orgasms belong to me." As soon as her body quit shaking he stood and shucked his pants and briefs, then looking at the corset, he made a motion for her to turn around.

"It's a bra on steroids," she laughed over her shoulder.

Tay unfastened the hooks, then massaged his hands over her ribs. "This didn't hurt you, did it?"

"See, you are the best. To answer your question, no. I'm fine, truly. Now, make love to me." She climbed up on the bed on all fours.

Knowing he wasn't going to last, he grabbed her by the ankle, and flipped her onto her back. "If you keep shaking that ass at me, I'm going to spank it." He fit his cock to the entrance to his own piece of heaven, then held both her hands in one of his above her head, and pushed inside in one hard thrust. She cried out at the same time as he groaned. She was made for him and literally stole his heart along with the breath from his lungs.

Her thighs gripped his hips, encouraging him to move. With her beautiful breasts on display below him, and her pussy holding him tightly, he began to thrust. She met him, grinding her pussy hard against his pelvis wanting that added friction, which he gladly gave.

He was in sensory over fucking load. Slanting his mouth over hers, welcoming her tongue into his

347

mouth, he sucked on it and groaned low when she sucked his into hers. He didn't think he could ever get deep enough or close enough, but he'd work for the rest of his life to try.

Lust, desire, need, and love all coiled tighter inside Tay, finally sending him over the edge at the same time he felt Jaqui's pussy gripping him tightly, squeezing every ounce of come he had to give until he had none left, and still the pleasure went on.

Jaqui stared up at him, owning him, body and soul. "Love you so much. To the moon and back," Tay said and rolled so he wouldn't collapse on top of her.

Breathless, she entwined her thigh between his. "Love you more."

He stroked his hand down her back, but didn't think anyone could love someone as much as he loved the woman in his arms.

# Epilogue

Nettie sat at Naughty Girls and pounded on the bar. "Give me another one." She held the empty shot glass up.

Traci filled the glass with another shot of tequila. "Girl, I'm not holding your hair."

She rolled her eyes, and tossed the shot back, no longer feeling the burn. "Men suck. I mean like big hairy donkey balls. I think I'm going to switch to the other team." She covered her mouth when she burped.

Her best friend's eyes widened. "Don't look at me, girl. I ain't going downtown to lady-town on nobody. Nope. I mean you're gorgeous, but I like men. Big strong men with big dicks." Traci held her hands apart, indicating the size she liked.

Several men seated around groaned.

"Come on Traci, that is not even natural," a cowboy said.

Traci shrugged. "Well, I'm just sayin. I can teach a cowboy with a big bull how to ride, but if he's got a small you know what…well, I just can't. The answer is no. I like big dicks and I cannot lie. You know the song, ladies."

Nettie sat up as the song in question began playing, a smile forming on her face. She and Traci both went to opposite ends of the long wooden bar, climbing up the stairs and grabbing a microphone one of the ladies behind the bar gave each of them. Nettie was pretty sure she was too drunk to maneuver so far off the ground, not to mention she was in a skirt that was too short, and any man seated on a barstool would get an eyeful. However, she'd had just enough to drink, her give a damn had done gone.

She'd just started on the chorus, when a familiar figure walked in. Shep Calhoun, the dirty, rotten, cheating bastard. Nettie ignored him and shuffled across the polished surface, dancing and singing, pretending like he didn't matter. Traci began bumping hips with her, mixing the words up with liking big cocks instead of butts, and then she heard her name being called.

Pretending she didn't hear him, Nettie turned her back to the room. The mirrored wall gave her a perfect view, defeating the purpose. Just when the song was about to end, the door opened, and a man walked in with two other men. Her mouth dried as she made eye contact with the first who entered. Good god, she didn't think she'd ever seen a man as handsome as the ones she'd met at Jaqui's wedding, even though she thought Shep was close, this man was right up there with them.

She watched his eyes narrow, then felt herself being pulled down. Fear had a scream ripping from her throat. Traci's yell was drowned out by the sound of her own heart beating double time, and then she was falling over Shep's shoulder.

"Put me down you fucker." She hit his back, looking around for someone to help her. Everyone there was scared of crossing the Calhoun's.

"Shut the hell up. I'm getting you out of here before you make any more of an ass out of yourself," Shep growled.

She wiggled, hitting him harder. "You are taking me nowhere. I'll call the cops. Put me down now. Traci, help me."

Traci came around the bar with a shotgun in her hand. "Put her down now, Shep, or I swear to my mama, I'll pepper your ass."

The sound of her best friend cocking her gun had her trying to get down, but the man holding her only tightened his hold. "You better think real hard, darlin. You don't want to make an enemy of me and my friends."

"I don't think the little thing wants to go with you. How bout you put her down, and I'll buy you a drink."

Nettie's body froze at the deep southern drawl. She tried to see who spoke, but Shep hit her so hard on her ass, it brought tears to her eyes, making her cry out.

"Damn, I guess we do this the hard way."

"Fucking-A, Roq. We're here not even a minute."

"I'll buy you a beer after we teach these boys how to treat a woman, Axl." Roq cracked his knuckles.

"Hell Yeah!" Axl cheered.

Roq knew without a doubt his friends had his back, and the little lady over the guy they'd called Shep, was not going to let go without a fight. He sighed and handed his Stetson to Axl. No way in hell was he going to get his favorite hat dirty or beat up in a bar fight.

**The End**

# Chapter One

"It's okay, little guy," Cora soothed, shoving down her fear for the little wolf caught in the illegal trap. The device had been hidden in a shallow crevice within a couple miles of her veterinary clinic. The way his wound was bleeding she knew, if she didn't get him free, he'd likely die. Inching closer to him, Cora watched for signs of aggression. "I'm going to get you out of there, but you have to promise not to bite me, okay?"

She squatted down until her face was almost level with his. "I'll try not to hurt you."

Cora swore it looked like the little guy nodded. At least Cora hoped that was a nod of agreement. His tiny body shook and shuddered. She prayed she wasn't mistaken.

After carefully looking over the contraption, she realized the jaws were meant for a much larger animal. Luckily for this wolf, his leg wasn't clamped between the steel jaws, only grazed. He was still stuck with his larger paw locked on the inside of the obviously modified bear trap and had a nasty gash that needed tending, sooner rather than later.

What seemed liked hours later, Cora finally got the device forced opened. Sweat trickling down her temples stung her eyes. The wolf lay panting like he'd just ran for miles. His gaze seemed to convey that he trusted her. Although it looked as though the trap only grazed his leg, she still checked to make sure it didn't break.

With a glance up at the darkening sky, Cora shrugged out of her jacket, leaving herself in only the yoga leggings and tank top she wore for her daily jog. South Dakota, during the day, could be warm, but as soon as the sun goes down, the temperatures drop dramatically. "Okay, little guy. I'm going to wrap you in my coat, and then I'm going to take you home with me."

Matching actions to words, she gently lifted his body. As she went to place his front right paw inside the jacket, the wolf howled the most pitiful whine, breaking her heart.

"I know it hurts, but I…" Cora jerked back in shock when the wounded animal bit down on her arm.

Once the wolf wriggled out of her coat, Cora watched in amazement as he licked her wound. If she didn't know any better, she'd swear he was apologizing, but thought that would be crazy. She gaped at him and scooted back a step or two, or three, until she stopped herself.

He whined again before trying to stand on his own, falling down when his front leg wouldn't hold him up.

Ignoring her own injury, she grabbed up her jacket and wrapped it around his body, being sure to pay close attention to his bleeding leg. "I know you're hurt, but try not to bite me again." She tried to sound stern when inside she was scared.

The walk back to her clinic took twice as long as normal since she didn't want to jar her patient any more than necessary. Every now and then his rough tongue would peek out and lick her arm. Although she was caught up on all her shots, she still worried about diseases from animals such as the wild wolf. At first glance she thought he was a baby wolf, now with him gathered in her arms and the couple of miles trek back to her home, she discovered he wasn't so young.

"Goodness, you must weigh close to seventy pounds, big guy."

Cora kept up a steady dialogue as she walked. When the clinic came into view, she nearly dropped to her knees in relief. Her arms shook under the stress of holding so much weight for such a long period of time. Normally, the hike would have taken her no time at all, but holding an injured animal that weighed almost as much as she did, the entire way was taxing, to say the least, not to mention the bite on her arm burned like fire.

She stopped outside the back door, adjusting her hold to punch in the code to unlock the back door, and, exhaling in relief, she murmured, "Thank you, technology." Cora's breathing was ragged by the time she made it inside.

Attached to the clinic was her small apartment, with a steel door separating the two spaces. Again, she punched in the code and then used her shoulder to enter the office area.

"Almost there, big guy. I'll have you fixed up in no time." Sweat poured down her chest, soaking her top. Cora ignored it all to focus on getting her patient fixed up. After she'd cleaned his wound, she found he had indeed broken his front leg, which was why he had probably bitten her when she moved him.

Thankful that her training kicked in to tend to the little wolf, when all she wanted to do was curl up in a ball and take a long nap, Cora placed the patched up wolf inside the padded kennel with a sense of relief. He whined when she attempted to lock the gate, his pain-filled gaze breaking her heart.

There were no other patients in the hospital area. She made the decision to leave the lock off, hoping she wasn't making a mistake and headed to take a bath.

Cora wiped her hand across the fogged mirror and stared at her own pain-filled gaze. "How can one little bitty bite hurt so damn much?" She looked at the freshly cleaned wound for what seemed like the thousandth time and stuck a thermometer in her mouth and waited for the beep, promising herself if her temperature was too high, she'd head into town.

Even after taking meds and a cool bath, nothing was bringing her temperature down. Looking at the triple digit reading on the tiny screen she cringed. There was nothing else she could do except head into town to urgent med. Cora really hated to go to the emergency room. She rolled her eyes and shook her head, stopping when the motion made her feel like she was on a tilt-a-whirl.

Wrapping a towel around herself, she decided to check on her patient one more time before she got dressed. The door between her home and the clinic was open, but the lights were out, sending a shiver of fear down her spine. Cora flipped the switch on the wall, illuminating the walkway. Her head felt heavy, the lights overly bright, making her stumble and lose her footing.

"Shit, damn." Rising to her feet, she reached her palm out to the wall to help steady herself and blinked a few times to bring things back into focus.

Standing in the middle of her clinic, with the injured wolf in his hands, was the most magnificent man she'd ever seen in her entire life. At over six foot tall, with short blonde hair and tattoos—lots of tattoos. The man exuded sex and menace. Yes, he definitely looked like he was angry. Even with her head feeling wonky, the sight of the unknown man made her body come alive. A whole different pulse began beating between her thighs, making Cora want to reach out and touch him, and not because she was in fear for her life.

"Who are you, and why do you have my wolf?" Cora was happy her voice didn't come out sounding as scared as she felt.

"Your wolf?"

The big man growled, the sound making her feel things she really shouldn't. Her nipples peaked at his deep rumble. Cora blamed the reaction on the fever.

"Listen, despite the fact you obviously broke into my clinic and I could press charges, I won't, but only if you put the animal down and leave the same way you came. You have less than five minutes, and then my offer is gone." Cora arched an eyebrow at him. "Do we have a deal?"

She waited for him to agree and put the sleeping wolf back down. Instead he quirked an eyebrow of his own, widened his stance, and sniffed the air.

In a move too fast for Cora to comprehend, the hunk standing a good ten feet away from her one moment, was all of a sudden crowding her space, sniffing her neck.

"Hey, have you heard of personal space?" When Cora attempted to push him back, her world spun.

* * * *

Zayn Malik didn't know whether to laugh or growl at the human who tried to tell him what to do, all while she stood in nothing but a miniscule towel. Holding his nephew in wolf form, he opted for the latter. Every member of their pack knew the rules, and he couldn't imagine Nolan, even at the young age of seven, breaking them. He'd wait until whatever drugs the woman gave Nolan wore off, and his nephew could shift back to find out what happened.

The overwhelming scent of antiseptic clouded his senses, making it hard for him to discern the unusual smells assaulting him. When she raised her hand to push him back, he watched her eyes roll back in her head. Zayn shifted Nolan to one arm, being careful of his injured leg, and caught the woman in his other arm.

That was how his alpha found him, holding an injured cub in one arm and a naked female in the other. It wasn't his fault the towel was dislodged when he pulled her into his arm to stop her from face planting onto the ceramic tile floor.

"You want to tell me why you are holding my cub and an unconscious naked human, Zayn?"

The smile his brother suppressed didn't make Zayn happy. He wanted to toss the human to Niall. Only fear of hurting his nephew kept him from following through on the thought. "Fuck off, Niall," he grumbled.

"Give me Nolan. Do we know what happened to him?" Niall reached for his cub, carefully tucking him into his body.

As he handed Nolan over to Niall, Zayn watched his brother grimace at the bandage on his son's leg, then sniff at the offending thing like he wanted to rip it off. The joking man was gone, replaced by the concerned father. Niall stood at over six foot three with more red in his blonde hair, but with the same blue eyes Zayn had. When Niall spoke as alpha, everyone in the pack listened. Although they had pack mates who were bigger than Niall, none could take him in a fight in human or wolf form.

They'd come to the Mystic River Pack in South Dakota when Niall found his mate by chance during one of their annual bike rides to Sturgis. Within a few months they'd found themselves full-fledged members of the pack, and Niall had learned he was to become a father.

His brother's nose then turned to the woman Zayn cradled in his arms. Niall's face got too close for Zayn's peace of mind to a bandage wrapped around her thin arm, making his inner wolf rumble close to the surface.

"Do you smell that?" Niall sniffed again.

"What?" Zayn pulled the woman closer to his chest, using his large hand to cover as much of her bare ass from his brother as possible.

The right side of Niall's mouth quirked up for a moment before he turned serious. He bent to pick up the towel that had been dropped and draped it over the female.

"She's been bitten."

Narrowing his eyes, Zayn ran his gaze over the sleeping woman. "What did you say?"

The woman in his arms stirred, a feverish light in her eyes. That was when he noticed she was extremely hot to the touch. The smell of the clinic and the medicines had masked the unmistakable scent of the marking, which meant his sweet little nephew had bitten the good doctor when she had obviously tried to help him.

"You smell soooo delicious." Cora licked her lips.

"Um, what's your name, sweetheart?" Zayn tilted his head back from her questing lips and tongue. *Damn, her tongue is really long.*

"Mmm. You taste really good too." Another wet swipe from her tongue had him panting.

"Oh, goddess. Baby, you need to stop." Zayn needed to get the woman to stop licking him or he was going to throw her down on the table and fuck her.

How the hell did she go from being cradled in his arms, to wrapped around him with her legs locked around his hips, and her arms around his head? Zayn swallowed. Jesus, he was ready to come in his jeans with his brother and nephew not five feet away.

"That's enough, Cora." The low timber of Niall's voice reverberated around the room. A shiver went through the woman in his arms, and she swung her stare toward his brother.

Niall held an ID card with a picture of the woman in his arms. The name, Dr. Cora Welch, was at the top for Zayn to see. His brother grinned, his blue eyes dancing with mirth.

* * * *

Cora's pussy contracted. Holy crap, the man was hot with a capital oh-my-lawd H, and she was humping him like a cat in heat, a naked cat in fricking heat.

She unlocked her ankles from the blonde Adonis's waist, hoping her legs would hold her up. They wobbled but didn't buckle—thankfully. "I'm so sorry…I don't know what came over me."

"I know what almost came all over me."

Sucking in a swift breath, Cora crossed one arm over her breasts and snatched the towel from the red haired man. Not that they hadn't seen everything there was to see, but she was in control of herself now.

"Smooth, Zayn, smooth. I apologize for my brother. He's not usually so crass, but we were worried when we couldn't find our little one here." He indicated the now alert wolf.

Eyes so blue peeked out between the big man's arms, accompanied by the whine she'd become accustomed to from the cub. She reached an unsteady hand toward his head to give a little scratch between his ears.

"Luckily for him, he's going to be okay. I found him stuck in a medieval looking animal trap made for a much larger animal. His little leg here," she indicated his cast, "barely missed being snapped in half by the steel jaws. I set the break and cleaned the wound. He should be right as rain in a few weeks."

Here she was buck-ass naked, carrying on a conversation with two men and a wolf. She was definitely sick. Cora raised her hand to feel her head. The short speech made her breathless, like she'd just run a marathon.

Behind her, she heard something growl. Turning to see the gorgeous man wearing a scowl, she took an involuntary step away. She looked around, fearing a wild animal had somehow gotten inside her office.

"Thank you, Cora Welch, for saving my cub. I owe you a life debt."

She swung her gaze back to the man holding the wolf. "Who are you? I've seen you in town, but I don't think we've met."

"I am Niall Malik. The man behind you is my brother, Zayn Malik."

Cora's tummy fluttered as she looked behind her at the man named Zayn. Lower down, between her thighs, her sex seemed to swell. A woman could come just from the stare of his blue eyed gaze.

"Well, it was very nice to meet you both, but I'm not feeling the best...so, um..."

Cora stumbled forward. A steely arm wrapped around her from behind. Blonde hair lightly dusted the arm roped with muscles upon muscles. Tattoos covered every available inch of skin she could see.

"Easy," Zayn murmured.

Cora blinked. Her stomach twisted; her pulse beat so loud she was sure even the man not holding her could hear it. Why did she feel like something monumental was about to happen?

"What the hell is wrong with me?"

Around her she saw white flashes. More men seemed to fill her once empty clinic. She wasn't a fan of having people witness her in a towel, let alone if she was going to either hump the man holding her or pass out. Either option seemed possible.

She blinked her eyes a few times to clear her vision. The newcomers pushed and jostled or shoved for prime position to see what the action was, making it the last straw for Cora. The equipment, along with all the instruments, was expensive, and not something she wanted to have to replace.

"Everyone stop!" Cora yelled, stepping forward with her hand out, hoping they didn't see the way it shook.

Zayn pulled her in closer to his body, eliminating the small space she'd attempted to put between them for her own peace of mind. Did the man not understand personal space?

Niall inclined his head. "You heard the lady. Everyone move out. The situation is in hand."

"Zayn's got something in hand."

"Watch your tone, McDowell." Niall warned.

McDowell was easily fifty pounds heavier than Niall, and it looked to be all muscle, but he seemed to shrink right before Cora's eyes at Niall's command. Cora studied all the men in front of her with a slow inspection. Faded denim hugged muscular legs, skin tight T-shirts or sleeveless flannel button down covered equally muscular torsos. Each man looked as if he stepped off the cover of some muscle magazine. She may be new to the Mystic River area, but she was pretty sure it was not normal for so many gorgeous men to be in one place, unless...*Oh please don't be gay.*

The extremely large erection digging into her back gave her hope that the man holding her wasn't, but in this day and age one just never knew.

"Sorry, Alpha. We see you found your cub." McDowell nodded towards Niall.

"Yes, let's head back. I'm sure he's tired from his long day."

Cora pulled her attention from checking out the bevy of gorgeous men to see the look of love shining in Niall's eyes as he looked down into the blue eyes of the wolf in his arms.

"Where did you say the trap was, Cora?" Zayn asked.

After she explained where it was located off the running trail, all the men in the room trained their eyes on her. "What are you looking at me like that for?"

"How did you get him back here?" Niall fired the question at her.

"I wrapped him in my jacket, picked him up, and carried him." Her arms still felt like Jell-O from carrying him for over two miles.

"You carried an injured, sixty-five pound cub, over two miles?' Zayn raised his brows.

Cora frowned. "Are you calling me a liar?" She spun out of his arms, nearly falling in her haste. She raised her hand when Zayn reached to touch her. "First of all, he weighs seventy-two pounds." She pointed to the cub in question. "Second of all, I usually run over five miles every day, not to mention I do yoga and cross-fit. So yeah, carrying him was really hard, and I nearly fell several times. My arms hurt just holding them up right now, but I did it, and I would do it again. I am not a liar. You and whoever else who don't believe me can go fuck yourself, and get the hell out of my clinic, because I'm tired, cranky, and I really need to lie down."

"Everybody back the fuck up." Zayn reached for her.

She took a deep breath. There were half a dozen men in the clinic, and she had no clue how they'd gotten in, or why they were all there. "Who are all of you, and why are you here? How did you get in?" The sound of distress from the cub stirred her overprotective instincts.

Forcing herself to turn her attention back to the man who seemed to be in charge, Cora smiled at the wide awake cub. "Did all that ruckus wake you up?"

Cora looked up into blue eyes very similar to the young wolf, but shook off the notion. "He may need some more pain meds. I had him on an IV drip, but *someone* took it out. I can give you some in pill form that you can mix in with his food if you notice him having any discomfort."

"Thank you, Cora. These are men from my...ah...family. When a cub goes missing everyone drops what they're doing to search. I'm sorry if we've scared you." Niall inclined his head.

She flicked away his thank you with a wave of her hand, glad to see almost everyone had cleared out, like they'd been waiting for the order. Now, if she could just get rid of the last of her unwanted visitors, she could go to bed. Surely by the time she woke up in the morning, she'd feel much better. If not, she'd go to the doctor, even if she hated the thought of that.

"Do you have someone to take care of you?" Niall asked.

"I don't need anyone taking care of me."

"I'm afraid I can't leave you here alone, Cora. Either you come home with us, or Zayn stays with you. We owe you a life debt."

"That's...that's crazy. I just saved your pet. Now you have him and everything is fine. I just have a bit of a cold. It's fine."

Niall shook his head, and Zayn's scowl deepened. "Seriously, I'm fine," she repeated.

"You coming with us, or is he staying here?"

He was an immovable obstacle. What do you do with an immovable obstacle? You go around him. Cora was glad her wits were still functioning, even though she knew her fever had to be even higher than the last time she took it.

"How about if I take some meds and call you in the morning?" See, she could be reasonable. She nodded.

"Did you grab her bag?"

With a quick glance, Cora gawked at the sight of Zayn holding her overnight bag with more than just a change of clothing. "Yes," Zayn growled.

"Good. Grab the girl."

What were the chances she could make it down the hall to her apartment with the steel door before either man could catch her? And if she did make it, could she get the alarm set and the police called before she passed out?

All these questions became a moot point when the man in front of her turned on his bare feet, which she just noticed, and walked out the front door, while Zayn murmured next to her ear, "You wouldn't make it two feet before I caught you."

"What?" Her voice came out in a breathless squeak she blamed on fright.

"You have very expressive eyes, and they were saying very clearly that you were about to do a runner. Rest assured, nobody, and I mean nobody in our…home would ever hurt you. We only want to see to your safety and wellbeing."

The last bit of strength Cora possessed left her all at once. Fortunately for her, Zayn just happened to be there to stop her from kissing the floor. Still, common sense told her she should let someone know where she was, just in case they planned to murder her—or something.

"I need to let my assistant know where I am in case of an emergency."

"It's Saturday. Aren't you closed on Sundays?"

Her challenge almost faded on her lips, not because she'd lost her senses, but because he'd bent his head so close to hers she could feel his breath on her lips. For a moment she almost forgot how to breathe. Holy buckets, the man was potent.

"I said in case of an emergency."

"Fine. Who do you need to call?"

Cora swallowed. Surely if they were going to kill her, they wouldn't allow her to let people know where she was going. Right?

With a grunt, Zayn waited while she left a voicemail for her assistant, letting her know she'd be staying with the Maliks and to call her cell if she needed her.

"Okay. You can put me down."

"Not gonna happen. You'll fall down, and then Niall will blame me."

Cora gaped at his audacity. "You can't carry me all the way back to your place."

"One of the guys brought my truck. I only have to carry you out front," he grunted.

She was too tired, and honestly too sick, to argue any further. Besides, his shoulder really felt good to lay her head on. "You smell really, really good."

"You said that before."

Cora closed her eyes against the flashes of white light.

Zayn pulled the door closed, engaging the locks. "Any problems on your way back, Kellen?"

"Coast was clear. Everything okay on your end, boss?" Kellen called from his place against the wall of the clinic.

At the sound of the newcomer's voice, Cora turned her head into Zayn's chest.

"Yes. Thank you for bringing my rig. Can you drive while I hold her? I don't think she will let me go long enough to let me drive us home."

She really wanted to lift her head and give him the finger, but at that very minute she couldn't. The steady rocking from his walk was so soothing her body went lax. Instead of fighting sleep, she let it claim her. A sense of security wrapped around her in the tattooed arms of the big man that she hadn't felt in a long time.

# About Elle Boon

Elle Boon lives in Middle-Merica as she likes to say…with her husband, two kids, and a black lab who is more like a small pony. She'd never planned to be a writer, but when life threw her a curve, she swerved with it, since she's athletically challenged. She's known for saying "Bless Your Heart" and dropping lots of F-bombs, but she loves where this new journey has taken her.

She writes what she loves to read, and that is romance, whether it's erotic or paranormal, as long as there is a happily ever after. Her biggest hope is that after readers have read one of her stories, they fall in love with her characters as much as she did. She loves creating new worlds and has more stories just waiting to be written. Elle believes in happily ever afters, and can guarantee you will always get one with her stories.

Connect with Elle online, she loves to hear from you:

www.elleboon.com

https://www.facebook.com/elle.boon

https://www.facebook.com/pages/Elle-Boon-Author/1429718517289545

https://twitter.com/ElleBoon1

https://www.facebook.com/groups/1405756769719931/

https://www.facebook.com/groups/wewroteyourbookboyfriends/

https://www.goodreads.com/author/show/8120085.Elle_Boon

**www.elleboon.com/newsletter**

# Author's Note

I'm often asked by wonderful readers how they could help get the word out about the book they enjoyed. There are many ways to help out your favorite author, but one of the best is by leaving an honest review. Another great way is spread the word by recommending the books you love, because stories are meant to be shared. Thank you so very much for reading this book and supporting all authors. If you'd like to find out more about Elle's books, visit her website, or follow her on FaceBook, Twitter and other social media sites.

# Other Books By Elle Boon

### Erotic Ménage
### *Ravens of War*
**Selena's Men**
**Two For Tamara**
**Jaklyn's Saviors**
**Kira's Warriors**

### Shifters Romance
### *Mystic Wolves*
**Accidentally Wolf**
**His Perfect Wolf**
**Jett's Wild Wolf**
**Bronx's Wicked Wolf, Coming Soon**

### Paranormal Romance
### *SmokeJumpers*
**FireStarter**
**Berserker's Rage**
**A SmokeJumpers Christmas**
**Mind Bender, Coming Soon**

### MC Shifters Erotic
### *Iron Wolves MC*
**Lyric's Accidental Mate**
**Xan's Feisty Mate**
**Kellen's Tempting Mate**
**Slater's Enchanted Mate**
**Bodhi's Synful Mate, Coming in 2016**